FIC   Havazelet, Ehud.

         What is it then
         between us?

$15•95

DATE			

What is it then
between us?

What is it then between us?

Stories by
Ehud Havazelet

Charles Scribner's Sons
New York

Fic

Charles Scribner's Sons
Macmillan Publishing Company
866 Third Avenue, New York, NY 10022
Collier Macmillan Canada, Inc.

This is a work of fiction. Names, characters, places, and incidents either are the product of the author's imagination or are used fictiously. Any resemblance to actual events or persons, living or dead, is entirely coincidental.

Library of Congress Cataloging-in-Publication Data

Havazelet, Ehud.
    What is it then between us?
    I. Title.   *Roo642 38819*
PS3558.A776W48   1988   813'.54   87-28897
ISBN 0-684-18919-4

10 9 8 7 6 5 4 3 2 1

Printed in the United States of America

To my mother and father

CONTENTS

What Is It Then Between Us?   1

Jillie   15

Resident   35

Glass   41

Solace   67

No Word for Mercy   81

What Everyone Wants   111

Natalie Wood's Amazing Eyes   145

The Only Thing You've Got   157

I would like to thank the Creative Writing Program at Stanford University and the University of Iowa Writers Workshop for fellowships which gave me the time to write these stories; to John L'Heureux, my thanks for his encouragement and guidance; and to Milla, who was with me through all of it, my gratitude and love.

WHAT IS IT THEN BETWEEN US?

What is it then between us?
What is the count of the scores or hundreds of years between
    us?

Whatever it is, it avails not—distance avails not, and place avails
    not,
I too lived, Brooklyn of ample hills was mine,
I too walk'd the streets of Manhattan island, and bathed in the
    waters around it,
I too felt the curious abrupt questionings stir within me,
In the day among crowds of people sometimes they came upon
    me,
In my walks home late at night or as I lay in my bed they came
    upon me,
I too had been struck from the float forever held in solution. . . .

—from "Crossing Brooklyn Ferry" by Walt Whitman

L ike this.
        I breeze through town and she takes me in. Call from
Chinatown, Port Authority, Yankee Stadium. Can I see you
now. Tonight. Arrive with flowers, a quart of Jack, Glenn
Gould playing Bach. The energy of the city square between
my shoulders, I seek the light of occasion in her eyes.

She has a man, now. She gets him out of the way. She
makes the bed and looks around the room, struck that its
casualness is just right—empty coffee mugs, poetry books
tumbled in a corner. She turns to me and says—all we need
is cool sheets, a bottle of wine, and Cary Grant on *The Late
Show*. We could go on forever. We will, I answer her. We
already have.

Then six blocks to the university. In the campus bar, they
still have jazz. We drink furiously and I make her laugh the
way no one can, bringing that sheen to the surface. I'm back
now, I tell her. I've got plans for us. I lean forward and smile.
I tease myself with her breasts but there is no need to touch

her; we are beyond urgency. It is a glorious return—back in the city, annealed, a beautiful woman to take me home, and only the vaguest memories of another night, fear drying the words on my tongue. Our earlier life plays about our table as formless and whimsical as smoke.

The doorman doesn't recognize me. An old man, he regards me with dim suspicion, says my name means nothing to him. He dials her on the house phone, keeping his eyes on me, brown eyes sifted through with gray, watchful.

A man down here, Miss. Says he knows you.

He hands me the phone and I dredge for the night I had planned—poetry and jazz, memorable times—but find nothing. I hold the phone to my mouth, his old man smell lifting off the plastic. I say hello into the receiver. I'm downstairs, I say. I just got in.

I listen to the swaying of phone sounds, a distant keening on the wire. The doorman reaches out. Just as he is about to take the phone, she says, four months. Where have you been four months?

North, I say. Around. I've been planning to call.

Four months. And before I can answer, she says, come up, then. I wouldn't want to keep you waiting.

I watch her sleep. In the blue before dawn with the curtains thick against the street, I am nothing more than the tip of my cigarette, its arc to my lips, its smolder and weave. I have swallowed just one more little beauty, because sleep was out of the question, because she didn't want me in her bed. I am calm, now. I can sit as long as I must. She moves in her sleep, an arm across empty sheets. The room is a high-ceilinged box, a chamber, a place to be sealed away. Everything is here,

4

everything we would need. I sit at the other edge and it is cold in her room. But she is there, under the blankets, mounding naked and silken in her dozing heat, ample, gathering strength. She does not want me in her bed but she will not make me leave. The curtains are thick and they hold off the light. I bring cigarettes to my lips and away again. They make sounds like small kisses in the dark.

I was born in this city. They don't hand out passports here. I conquered it, assaulting it from all sides, laying siege from the boroughs, plotting my approach. I climbed the Empire State, the Chrysler, the Riverside Church, and I saw it from the skies. I crossed the Williamsburg and the Willis Avenue, and looked down at the roiling gray water. I stood on the Palisades in another state taking in the island whole with one flex of my neck. I rode the subway to the end of the line, the end of all the lines—South Ferry, Coney Island, Pelham Park, 179th Street in Bayside, Queens. I knew the tubular caverns and freight elevators of the uptown IRT, and the endless underground miles of Grand Central. I knew the tunnels where the winos slept, the bag ladies, and the hole in the Flushing Line wall where you could see rats streaming like cells in the blood. I could recite the skyline, eyes closed, knew a fountain in Central Park deserted and completely overgrown, and I understood how Times Square beat back the night almost to extinction. I rode this city like Triton rides the waves and I never should have left. My one question for you. Why would I ever want to leave?

In the Ansonia, Harry and I count out beauties over bottles of beer. Roland Kirk is on the stereo, as always, and there are speakers all over the room—by the windows, concealed in

closets, on stray chairs and overturned boxes—so the sound
does not emanate, does not travel, simply is, everywhere at
once. Roland Kirk was a hero, a master of circular breathing,
which means he had evolved to a state where he was breathing 100 percent of the time, alive that way every moment,
until his body gave out from joy and exhaustion, you would
have to believe. Roland Kirk could play an alto and a tenor at
the same time and in harmonies much stiffer than simple
thirds. We saw this, at the Bottom Line, the loft on Second
Avenue. He could then put a penny whistle in each nostril
and blow there too, he could play out of his ears, legend had
it, but the union clamped down on this, and then his manager,
who wanted to harness a good thing, and then his doctors, in
simple honest fear. When Roland Kirk died at forty-one, after
a stroke and heart trouble, his body closing down in pieces,
there were spontaneous processions all over the island, people
needing to walk, to get outdoors, to look around for themselves. Radios played in every window, out of cars and restaurants, and for a day, an afternoon, perhaps, all of Manhattan
spoke the same new language.

Harry slits the skin of a beauty with his thumbnail and
pours the bitter powder on his tongue. His smile is horrible as
the crystals work around his mouth.

Have you seen her, he says.

Sure, I say. First thing.

What did you tell her?

That I'm back. We're all gonna be okay, I told her.

Harry looks at me. He palms beauties into a paper sack.
He punches numbers into a calculator. Around us, Roland
Kirk soars, unceasing, and I have to work for a part of Harry's
attention.

I remember when you moved in this place, I tell him. Stokes' wedding cake, you called it, Harry. Babe Ruth had lived in this very apartment, you said, Caruso across the hall. You told me Heifetz was on the thirteenth floor, blind and nobody knowing it, and that Isadora Duncan used to come Tuesday afternoons to see a Rumanian who never left his apartment. You told me these things, Harry, I say. Would you deny that now?

Harry punches in more numbers, writes on a yellow pad. Roland Kirk has abandoned the melody and his accompanists are left behind to tap out rhythms. Roland Kirk hears notes he has never heard before.

There's more, I say to Harry. You told me apartment 14-B has been sealed off by the police until the year 2000. You told me the walls are three feet thick and neighbors could only guess what went on at Maria Callas's, nights the mayor was seen outside her door, the governor, the ambassador from Mexico City. Don't tell me now you didn't say these things, I tell Harry. I remember.

Harry has finished his calculating. He sweeps crystal off the tabletop and smears a thumb across his gums. He pushes the bag over and points out what I owe. I am standing, trying to get above the sound, but Roland Kirk finds me there, too.

Harry says, you remember a lot.

Everything, I say. All of it.

Me, I remember just a thing or two, he says, and the look on his face is not of a friend. I am pulling bills out of my pocket, grabbing the paper bag, searching for the door. I remember a phone call, almost morning, Harry says, a certain girlfriend of yours. Did I know where you were. Did anybody know where you were. I remember a taxi ride uptown, Harry says, and he has followed me into the hallway, halfway to the bank of elevators. I remember we went to your place, he calls out, she was afraid what she would find so I went along. I remember the place was empty, Harry shouts, his voice ringing through me in the deep stairwell. The lights were out and you were gone. That's what I remember.

The Ansonia Hotel was built in 1903 by William Earl Dodge Stokes, an eccentric with money to burn. Originally planned for twenty stories, construction was halted at sixteen, when Stokes decided that was the height at which he preferred to live. To evade the city fire insurers, Stokes instructed the builders to make the terra-cotta walls thirty-six inches thick, to lace the edifice with dozens of intricate connecting balconies, to install extra plumbing and water supply. The Ansonia immediately became a favorite among artists, musicians and celebrities, people who, for one reason or another, required insulation from the world outside. On the roof, Stokes raised chickens and goats, selling the eggs to his tenants at a discount, keeping the goat milk for a diet he had adopted while traveling once in the Orient. To run the two fully stocked restaurants, he lured Chef Gurnsey Webb away from the Plaza Hotel. Many older celebrities still keep apartments in the building, and though its fortunes have declined somewhat— the restaurants have given way to a shoe repair and a Chinese laundry, and the lobby is home to many whose business there is uncertain—its distinctive finials and cupolas, the delicate latticework of its balconies, the matching towers and the astounding detail of its facade still rise above the subway lines on Seventy-second Street and draw the eye of the curious and those given to infatuation.

In the lobby, I stand in shadow and collect my thoughts. I clench my hand around the bag in my pocket, try to formulate plans. A man has been sleeping against the far wall and he opens his eyes to watch me. I take a step toward the door. The lobby has only weak bulbs high in the ceiling and their light is dim, aqueous. The marble walls are so thickly veined they seem to pulse and for a moment I think I feel the old building shift and settle above me in respiration. The door at the end of the lobby is a bright rectangular plane. Outside, taxis careen and truck drivers open their mouths to shout. The man gets up from the floor and walks over. He reaches a hand out to me and I put a shoulder into him, hard, and head for the exit, but again I stop, just a step or two short. I watch the glass doorframe where fast shapes and men's voices contend in the violent light.

In other days, Central Park was grassland and the animals roved wild. There were gaslights on the avenues and a garden in Madison Square. There was a reservoir on Forty-second Street like a vanquished pyramid, and on a Spanish tower, Diana raised her bow at the heavens. I tell her these things. Listen, I say. Please, I say. I know a woman on Park Avenue who keeps geraniums in bloom through the winter, moss roses, peonies, lily of the valley. In Washington Square, I tell her, Minetta Brook bubbles an arm's length from the surface. I know a man who spins the water through a tube in his basement. He would show you. Please.

We are in her room with the curtains wide, the sun blasting up against the windows. I waited hours on her doorfront, away from the old man, and when she saw me, she made a slight hesitation, as if she might turn the corner again, head crosstown or to the park. But I called out. I ran to her and she let me follow her upstairs.

While I talk, she dresses, making ready to leave. I talk quickly, holding her there until the right words form, pausing only a moment, discreetly, to slip a beauty under my tongue, precise consolation. She looks at me once in a while. She changes her shirt right there, puts a skirted leg on a chair to buff a shoe, but there is no seduction in these movements. She would do the same if she were alone. When she is done, she stands in front of the chair where I sit.

Is that what you came to tell me? she says. Stories? A history lesson?

No, I say. More. Much more.

Drop in after months to discuss the city that never was, is that it?

No, I say. Wait. Listen.

You wait, she tells me, and walks closer until the blue weave of her skirt presses hard against my knees. You listen. I don't live in that world. I never heard of that city. I'm not acquainted with sports heroes, potentates, figures out of legend. In my world, it's a good day if the buses run on time, you come out of the subway without some stranger's fingerprints all over your body. In my world, drunks swerve across the median doing ninety, terrorists from a country you've never heard of carry machine guns into the restaurant where you're trying to have a quiet meal. In my world, she says, you get by, you try to, and people are accountable. You want to hear about my world? She takes my face in her hands, brings it up sharply. You ran, she says. It was your party, your friends. Influential people, a town house in Riverdale. Open your mind, you said, grow, you said, and it was fine as long as they left me alone. But not later. He got me in a corner, I was frightened, and what do you say? Be nice, it's his place. I said I wanted to leave. I looked right at you and said I wanted to go. But you weren't watching me. I was begging you. What's going to happen here, I said, but you

10

weren't looking at me, you were looking at him, this dealer, this important person, this sleazy old man with his hand up your lover's thighs. And you didn't go for some air, or for a final blow with the boys around the pool. You ran. You left me there and ran out of town, out of my life. You're nothing, she says to me, and lets my face drop from her hands. You're not even here.

In the first New York blackout, Kevin Simmons was a small boy in Queens, angry at his mother. He took his Tom Tresh Louisville Slugger and gave every streetlight on his block a solid whack. They rang like church bells. When he whaled into the last one, all the lights in the city went out. He went to the police then, by himself, and told them he was surprised, but he couldn't say he was sorry.

When the banks foreclosed on Eugene's grandfather, between the wars, the old man closed up shop in the middle of the day. He brought the truck around back and loaded it full as could be. He drove to City Hall, where he covered the steps and half the lawn with bread and sausages, pasta, pickled foods in great yellow jars, canned goods, eighty dozen eggs. It made the papers. When La Guardia arranged a postponement for Eugene's grandfather, he told the reporters, "What else was I going to do?"

Steve Brodie was the first to survive leaping off the Brooklyn Bridge. They made a Broadway play based on his life. Though it was soon revealed he had never actually gone through with the jump, it was a hero's world then, and he was a famous and happy man to the end of his days.

One summer, before the gas wars, Lucky Linda disappeared into Harlem. Get me another one of these, she told me. I'll be right back. Okay, I said, what are they? It doesn't matter; she was in the doorway by then, and in the half-light, she was already losing form. It doesn't matter. Something cool in a tall glass.

My moment is brief, diminutive by these standards. I leave her for the second time, the final time, and I wander. I stockpile little beauties, I collect on some old debts, establish a few new ones. I think of going to the Cloisters or Battery Park on sunny days, and I assume I will, I assume I will. It is night on Fulton Street when my moment arrives. I have been eating only beauties for days, too many perhaps, until everything threatens to fuse into long skeins of silver and black, loops of orange and aquamarine. They illuminate the sky at night now, the Empire State, green and red for Christmas, blue and white for the World Series. The Chrysler is an elaborate spear to snag careless angels. The city exults in light.

I hear it as if I have heard it countless times. How long has she been calling, "Stop that man. Somebody do something." He flashes by me, quick. The knife gleams. The knife actually gleams. I run before I can question myself. He looks over a shoulder and I swear, he laughs. He lopes, without effort, but I am in his wake, I am considering leaving my feet altogether.

We turn down alleyways, into streets where the moon reaches only rooftops and upper-story windows. I am gaining no ground but I am holding firm, attached to him and he knows it. He can go nowhere without me. I empty into my eyes, my legs, my lungs, like a star exploding. He turns onto the FDR exit ramp; I follow, mesmerized, adoring. Over his shoulder again, I see the knife. We run onto the highway. Ahead of us, car lights, endless, are rows of teeth in Leviathan's jaw. He skips into the center lane and heads uptown, against traffic, daring me to follow. I follow. We run toward the lights, toward midtown and the Bronx, Hudson Bay and the Arctic, until our hearts stop, until we are swallowed clean, entire.

JILLIE

I have a photograph of Jillie from that summer. Lank blond hair and the thin angling legs of a girl not quite thirteen. One hand up against the sun, her eyes blur into shadow and her lips are just opening, to smile or to speak. It is an old photograph and I have not kept it well. In the background, the top of the garage has been sheared away, and cracks run crosswise throughout the print. The scar on Jillie's face looks remarkably like one of these, a pale blue seam reaching from the wisps of hair by her ear to the delicate curve of her jaw and disappearing.

It was taken the day of a barbecue. The plates were not yet gathered and my father announced he would take pictures. My mother bent over Grandmother and began fixing her face. Sandra, Jillie's mother, took a mirror from her purse and dabbed at the cocoon of hair piled above her head. Jillie was standing in front of the garage when my father called her name. Lifting a hand to her eyes, she turned into the sun just as the shutter snapped.

*   *   *

Sandra was my mother's sister, younger by six years. She met and married Pete, over my parents' objections, while living in their house, in what was to be my room. They simply came in one night and announced they were moving to Ohio, where Pete had landed a job. Sandra was wearing a pearl necklace and a new coat. They hadn't meant not to invite my parents, Sandra said. It had just been one of those spur of the moment things. Pete stood by the window drinking a beer as Sandra showed them her ring. He was a tall sturdy man with thick red hair down to his shoulders. His blue eyes were lively, except when he was drinking, and they gave him an expression of almost constant amusement. When my mother walked up and told him he had better take care of her sister, he smiled at her and said he guessed he could do that all right.

Pete worked in auto parts in Youngstown. When Jillie was born they sent pictures, and for my birth, a miniature leather football with my name tooled across the stitches came by parcel post. They were supposed to visit Christmases, and one year, a joint vacation on the Gulf of Mexico was discussed, but the plans never came through. Sometimes, my mother had long conversations with Sandra on the phone.

Jillie remembered the first time Pete hit her mother. She heard the arguing from her bedroom, the voices rising to such a pitch that she sat up in bed. When the sound of Pete's hand on her mother's face stung in her ears, she held her breath and pulled up the covers. When the door slammed and she knew her father had gone, she stayed under the blanket anyway, feeling her breath warm the air around her.

The summer before Jillie was thirteen, Pete and Sandra had a fight. On the second day of a spree, Pete grabbed Jillie and put her in the car. He drove fast and talked about Sandra in a way that made Jillie close her eyes and try not to listen. She did not see the swerve of the front wheels, or the fence they broke through, or the tree. Pete was unconscious for twenty-four hours with a concussion and broken ribs. Jillie was not seriously injured, but glass from the windshield sliced into her face.

Sandra took Jillie from the hospital before the plastic surgeon could examine the girl, and drove eighteen hours to my parents' house. When my father opened the door onto a mild summer night, she was shaking. "I'm not going back this time," she said. "I swear I'm not." Jillie stood behind her, her face swollen and discolored under the bandages. She hesitated on the threshold for several seconds before coming in and letting my mother embrace her.

That summer, I don't think I knew I was in love with Jillie. I was a shy twelve-year-old. But I knew a center had come into my world. I spent hours looking at Jillie when I thought she didn't know; I found myself thinking of how she would react before I laughed or grew angry. And I stared at her scar, which flared red and seemed to divide her face in two.

I showed Jillie my secrets. I showed her the hole toward the back of the garage ceiling, hidden by the dark and planks of wood. We climbed through and sat by the small window in the garage's peak. I took her to the blue house, where birds lived in a pipe by the roof. We waited in the bushes and counted eight birds one after another—squeeze out, flutter and fly—like pinwheels in the wind. In the park, I showed her the painted outline of a body on the asphalt and we stood for some moments in silence, staring at the place a dead person had lain.

In the afternoons, our mothers would go shopping, or to the beauty parlor to lift Sandra's spirits, and Jillie and I would stay with Grandmother. After her second stroke, Grandmother could move nothing except her eyes. The doctor told my father it was questionable if she even saw with those eyes anymore; it might be a passive response to light and shadow, the doctor said.

Some days, we put Grandmother in her wheelchair and took her to the back porch. Jillie said she liked it in the sunshine and the air, and I was always ashamed to say I thought the doctor was right, that she didn't know what she liked or disliked anymore. There were cherry trees in the yard, and in late summer, robins pecked among the black hulls of decomposing fruit, and the air was heavy and sweet.

One day, Jillie put a basket of cherries in Grandmother's lap. After a few moments, a robin landed on the gate in front of her and then hopped into the basket on her knees. The bird wrestled with a bit of fruit and stretched a thin white worm from it. I giggled and looked nervously at Jillie.

"We shouldn't do that," I said.

"She likes it, can't you see?" Jillie said, not turning from Grandmother. There was now a bird in her lap and another on her shoulder. "She's the kind of lady who likes the birds."

Other days, we stayed with Grandmother in her room. Jillie sat on the large four-posted bed and took one of Grandmother's hands, turning it over, stroking it, running her fingers up the raised blue veins. "Look. Aren't they beautiful?" Jillie would ask me. Jillie would say, "Do you want me to dance, Grandma?" and I would look closer at Grandmother's face because Jillie said she would answer, though I never saw how.

Taking a shawl or the frilled coverlet off the bed, or sometimes just wrapping herself in and out of her long bright hair, Jillie would dance. There was no music as Jillie wove her arms slowly through the air or whipped them about in wild leaps; just Jillie's feet on the wooden floor and her quick hoarse breathing.

She never asked me if I wanted to dance, though I'm certain I wouldn't have. As she veiled fingers across her face or flung her legs before her, she kept her blue eyes on Grandmother: watching. She was dancing for the old woman. And those other eyes, faded, pendent with tears that would not flow—I came to believe those eyes saw Jillie dance.

In the loft over the garage, I would rub Jillie's back until we were called to dinner. At midday, the sun burned at the holes in the roof, but toward evening, light angled softly through the dusty window and the world looked muted and far away.

Jillie lay on her stomach and I pulled the sweatshirt up, over the downy groove where the skin was softest, stopping at the rounded slopes of her shoulders. I brought my fingers up slowly, rippling the flesh and then passing. Sometimes I would rest my hand on the small of her back when her breathing became still, and sometimes I lay down beside her and stared at the roof, pierced by tiny spots of sun.

"When we live together," Jillie said, "it won't be any place like this."

"Where will it be?" I asked.

"Someplace high up, in the snow. Someplace it would take days to get to and most people wouldn't even try. It would be white, like the snow, and you couldn't even see it except for the smoke from the chimneys."

"What would we eat?"

"Whatever we found. We would trap things and kill them."

"Rabbits?" I said. "Squirrels?"

She nodded. I looked up at the rafters and tried to picture what was in Jillie's mind. I tried for the snow; the cold sharp air; the building white against white, vanishing into itself. The image shimmered in my mind and faded. I felt lonely.

"And will we come back here at all?" I asked her.

Jillie turned her head toward me. Her eyes reflected the sinking light like an animal's in the dark.

"No," she said. "This place will be gone."

On the day Grandmother died we sat in the kitchen while the doctor drank his coffee. He was a small man in a dark suit and he held the coffee cup inches from his face, as if wanting its warmth.

"You like to see them go that way," he said. "They don't even know it at the end."

In our holiday clothing, Jillie and I sat with Grandmother. The light was dim through the drawn shades. I sat in a chair by the bureau, conscious of the pressure of my necktie. Jillie stood by the bed, the heel of one black shoe on the toe of the other, her white dress faintly luminous in the midday twilight.

"Do I look like her, you think?" she asked me. I was startled by her voice. I rose. From closer, I could not make myself suppose Grandmother was resting. She seemed impossibly heavy, skin sagging in folds against her face. I saw no relation between the body in the bed and Jillie, white dress and shiny shoes, leaning forward as if she might, at any second, begin to float.

"No," I said. "She's old."

Jillie moved closer and tried to hold one of Grandmother's hands. She could not move it. "Jillie," I said. She reached out a hand, rested it on Grandmother's forehead, and pinched an eye open with her thumb. The skin pulled away and the eye—solid, dry and lusterless as bone—stared in fixed surprise at the ceiling.

I heard myself say Jillie's name, and felt her shoulder warm beneath her dress.

On Jillie's birthday, we had a party after dinner. My mother baked a chocolate cake with Jillie's name on it and my father bought a bottle of champagne. Sandra gave Jillie a pair of turquoise earrings and promised to take her downtown to have her ears pierced the following week.

Sandra drank a lot of champagne, and when my father put a record on the phonograph, pulled me into the center of the room to dance. She pressed my head against her dress and the sweetness of her perfume mixed with the sour smell of the champagne as she sang into my ear. Her breasts were heavy against my cheek and I was embarrassed to be considered so young that I could be held to them like a child. After the music, we sat at the table. Sandra was still singing. She put her arms around Jillie.

"Oh, honey," she said, "you're getting to be so beautiful, your own mother will be jealous soon." She smiled. "When I get the money, baby, I promise. We'll fix that horrible thing on your face."

The phone rang in the kitchen and my father talked in a low voice. Sandra was winding Jillie's hair above her head when his voice became louder. "I'm not sure she *would* like to," we heard him say.

Sandra's eyes, which had been wandering, became alert. "Who is that?" she said to my mother. "Who's on the phone?"

My father came into the room. "It's Pete," he said. "You don't have to talk to him."

Sandra rushed past him into the kitchen. We could hear her sobbing. Jillie picked up one of the earrings and rubbed it between her fingers. Sandra hung up the phone and walked in.

"Pete's in town," she said. "He's coming over."

"We won't let him in the house, Sandra," my mother said.

"He wants to see Jillie. It's her birthday."

Pete arrived in a sport jacket and tie. His hair was in a neat ponytail and he carried flowers and a six-pack of beer. He stood in the doorway smiling. Sandra stood at the table.

"Sandy," Pete said.

She ran to him and they kissed. Pete walked in with Sandra on his arm. My father nodded stiffly at him and my mother went into the kitchen.

"Honey," Sandra said. "Say hello to your father."

"Hello, Daddy," Jillie said.

Pete said, "I've come for your birthday, baby. Did you think I'd miss that?"

Jillie walked over and Pete put his free arm around her. Pressed into his large body, she looked very young. Her eyes, clear and insistent, seemed to focus on something far away.

In my room that night, I heard the sounds of an argument. There was my father's voice trying to remain civil, my mother's with a shrill note of pleading, Pete's casual drawl, always as if a laugh were gathering just below the surface, and Sandra's wail, lifting slowly.

The front door slammed and Sandra began to scream. My father shouted and I heard my mother breathing as she climbed the stairs to her room. My father said something to Sandra, and his tone had a finality that prevented any answer. I heard his heavy feet on the stairs, and as I fell asleep, Sandra's whimpering into silence, alone.

24

*   *   *

In the loft the next day, I found Jillie with a sleeping bag and a basket of food.

"She's going back to him," she said. "They want to take me with them."

I looked at her face. In the shadows, the scar reached out of her hair like a long bony finger. I looked at the sleeping bag and the food, and nodded.

"I'm staying here. You'll bring me food and empty that can at night. You can only come up here at night."

"It'll get cold, Jillie."

"I took your father's sleeping bag. They don't know about this place, do they?"

"I don't think so. Nobody uses the garage."

She looked around. The events of the night before and Jillie's announcement upset me more than I could tell her, and in any case, I knew I would help.

"How long will you stay here?" I asked.

She was startled. "I don't know," she said. "A few days." She sat on the sleeping bag.

"I have something for you."

She smiled. "What?"

"A birthday present." I handed her the album cover I had brought with me. Inside was a collage cut from magazines and travel posters. A white wooden house with light blue shingles sat on a snow-covered mountain. There were fruit trees and sea birds and a pointed sun-face wearing dark glasses. To the side, Arctic hares ate leaves and brambles. "Our place," I said.

"It's perfect," she said. "I'll look at it all the time."

That evening, Jillie did not come home for dinner. Sandra kept lighting cigarettes and leaving them unsmoked all over the house. I had already said I knew nothing, but when my mother walked in to say the last of the neighbors had not seen Jillie, Sandra looked wildly at me. "He knows," she said. "He knows where she's gone. Make him say."

She grabbed my shoulders and shook me, her fingernails deep in my skin. I remembered Jillie saying if you're going to get hit, start to cry, and they'll feel sorry for you. It's not hard, she had said. Crying is a lot like laughing. To my surprise, a thin cry escaped my mouth and tears started down my cheeks.

"Leave him alone, Sandra," my mother said. "Can't you see he's as upset as we are?"

Sandra called Pete at the hotel and they drove around the neighborhood together. The police came and my mother gave them the photograph of Jillie in front of the garage. I was sent to bed.

At breakfast, Pete was in his undershirt, making a list of the people Jillie knew. He asked me where we used to go, if we had any favorite spots. I told him we didn't. He looked at me, and I felt a pressure build in my throat. It was harder, somehow, to lie to Pete. I thought he would accuse me right then, but he looked away and asked for more coffee.

All day, my parents were on the phone. I looked around for things to bring Jillie that night and tried to draw as little attention as possible.

Jillie was wrapped in the sleeping bag. I could barely make her out.

"How's it going?" she asked.

"Okay. They're upset. I'm worried about your father."

"Is he drinking?"

"A little."

26

My eyes grew accustomed to the dark. I had never been in the loft at night before.

"Spooky in here," I said.

"No, it isn't. It's nice. Look." She pointed at one of the walls. Halfway up, wedged between two nails, was the collage I had given her.

"It's kind of cold," I said.

"Come in here."

We sat under the sleeping bag for a few minutes and then Jillie said I should go. They might wake up and look for me.

"Where's the can?" I asked.

"Near the hole. You probably stepped in it."

"I see it. You want anything special?"

"Yeah. Peanut butter."

I stood up.

"Thanks," she said, and stood near me. She leaned over and kissed my cheek.

"You're a dumb bitch," Pete said, looking at Sandra blankly. "You never should have been a mother."

"Me," Sandra said. "Who do you think she's running from?"

"She's crazy as you are. Two crazy bitches."

Pete had been drinking since early morning. He sat at the table pouring whiskey slowly into a water glass, holding it momentarily before his lips and then drinking it down in big unhurried swallows. He had been silent an hour before speaking to Sandra.

"Well," he said. "We find that kid and I'll fix her."

Sandra stood in the doorway to the kitchen. "Yeah, Pete," she said. "You fix her. Why don't you take her for another ride?" Pete filled a glass with whiskey. "Big fucking guy," she said. "Why don't you finish your bottle and beat me up?

My sister's never seen you do it. Why don't you beat her too? Beat up everyone and then disappear for a month." Sandra's voice was getting higher. She leaned against the doorframe and her head bobbed with the force of her breathing.

"You better shut up now," Pete said.

My mother took Sandra by the shoulder and led her into the kitchen. My father sat down opposite Pete.

"What a dumb bitch," Pete said, looking away.

It had been a chilly day, gray clouds hanging flat against the sky, and toward evening it began to rain, a steady careening rain that hissed off the sidewalks. When I went to bed, it had not let up. I waited two hours and slipped out, carrying a blanket and a large poncho.

I climbed into the garage by a side window. Water fell steadily from the ceiling and collected on the cement floor. I climbed through the hole, almost losing my balance on the slick wood.

"Jillie," I whispered.

"Hi," she said. I sat without moving, waiting to see. Rain whipped at the roof above and the air smelled of wet dust and rotting wood. After a few moments, I could distinguish the outlines of the walls, and here and there, a downward shimmering where water slid on them in sheets. Jillie was in the far corner, wrapped in the bag. Her hair hung in limp strands.

"Are you all right?"

"Yeah," she said. "I got a little wet."

I had to slosh through an inch of water to reach her. The sleeping bag oozed like a sponge.

"It's freezing in here, Jillie," I said. "Maybe you should come down." She didn't answer. "I brought a blanket," I said, "and a poncho. Is the sleeping bag all soaked?"

"Just the bottom. It's dry up here."

We listened to the rain. There was a clarity to that sound I have not forgotten—each drop sharp against the shingles, distinct, though identical to the rest. It was soothing.

Jillie said, "Help me. It was so hot before, I let my clothes get wet."

She folded the sleeping bag in half and lined it with the blanket. She draped the poncho over the bag. The spot she had chosen was the highest on the floor, the roof above it nearly whole. The makeshift bed would be relatively dry.

"There," she said, when she had finished.

She stood up and began taking off her clothes. I could almost feel the shiver as her skin opened to the damp. Her clothing slapped to the floor. Moving fast, her pale body shifting before me like clouds before the moon, she crawled into the bag.

"Is it okay?" I asked.

"Oh, it's warm."

I sat by the edge of the bed. The rain seemed to be subsiding. It rose and fell against the roof, breathing, almost.

"Jillie," I said. "I want to stay."

"All right," she said. "There's room."

My clothes were slimy with the muck I had crawled through. I pulled them off quickly and slipped in beside Jillie. Her skin shocked against mine, first cool and smooth, then warmer. She pulled the bag over us and turned toward me. There was room enough only if we pushed together. We put our arms around each other and my hands, as if automatically, began stroking her back. Her fingers drew me close lightly. My lips brushed her face and I began kissing her, softly, as if I would never stop, her nose, her cheek, her mouth, her eyes.

29

I heard the rain moved by the wind and my short breaths between kisses.

It was just light. The rain had ended and isolated dripping sounds mingled with bird calls. I felt sweat on Jillie's skin and her face was warm. She sneezed, and from the slight glaze in her eyes, I could see she was feverish.

She made me hurry. I dressed and looked at her shuddering in the bag.

"You're sick."

"Hurry," she said.

I don't know if my decision was made then or if it formed slowly through the morning. I have never been able to conclude that I even made a decision, with the weighing of choice, of consequence. But I know that Jillie's face was in my mind all morning.

My mother stood by the window in the kitchen, drinking coffee.

"She's in the garage, Mom."

"What?"

"Jillie is."

"What are you saying? Where?"

"In the garage. She's sick."

I sat at the table and heard the noises and shouting. When Pete carried Jillie in, Sandra walked up to me and slapped me hard across the face.

My ears filled with ringing and I turned quickly toward Jillie. She was looking at me. I felt my mouth opening, and then her eyes became dull, solid. She looked away.

Jillie was in bed three days and she didn't want to see me. The night after she was found, Pete and Sandra and my parents had a long talk. By the end, both Pete and his wife were crying.

When Pete loaded the car to leave, Jillie was on the sofa, wrapped in a blanket. She still had a fever, but they wanted to get her home. I had climbed up to the loft before my father boarded it shut and taken the collage of the house in the snow. I gave it to Jillie.

"What's that?" Sandra said brightly.

"It's just a place," I said, looking at Jillie. "A house."

"Oh," Sandra crooned. "Did you make it?"

"Yes. For Jillie."

"That's nice," Sandra said. "I'm sure she's very grateful."

Jillie did not look at me. Pete came in with a box of candy and a huge rag doll. There was kissing and hugging and talk about Christmas. Pete gripped my shoulder and gave me a steady look by which I suppose he meant he forgave me. Sandra rumpled my hair and left a waxy imprint of lips on my cheek. We went out to the car and waved until it turned the corner. In the house, Jillie had left the collage on the sofa.

Some time later, the police returned the photograph of Jillie to my parents. For years it has been bundled, along with the snow collage, in a box full of poems, love letters, and other tokens which are supposed to stay forgetfulness.

I have seen Jillie since. Though we did not see her family, over the years, I heard news of her: Jillie had moved away without finishing school, had wired from Mexico for money, had been in trouble with the law. When I was eighteen, she was to have come to the wedding of a distant cousin, and I took the train overnight to Buffalo, but she had called to say she couldn't make it. My cousin didn't know why.

I had heard of her marriage and, vaguely, of children.

When my job required that I drive out west, I realized I would be passing the town in which she lived. I resisted all thoughts of a visit. That summer was long past, but it was still familiar to my mind, sometimes as if I could accommodate only that single memory.

But on the day of the drive, something in the late afternoon light moved me. It was summer again, and the sky ahead threatened rain. I had been driving since early morning, and suddenly the thought of driving through the night in another rainfall to another motel was too much to bear. A quick phone call, a short detour, and I stood in Jillie's home.

Her blond hair was clipped and she wore sunglasses like her mother had. A surgeon had repaired her scar and her young woman's face was without blemish, though more sharply angled than I remembered it. The children were away, she told me. They would be so disappointed.

We sat in the living room and drank beer. I met her husband, whose resemblance to Pete was so strong that I found it hard to look at him. From the way he grasped my hand and said, "So here's the famous cousin I've heard so much about," I knew he had never heard a word about me.

We talked briefly about that summer, and Jillie's husband loosed his hearty booming laugh several times at our adventure. They asked about my business; they expected a wedding invitation soon. When they asked me to stay for dinner, I said no, I had friends awaiting me on the Coast.

Before I left, Jillie kissed my cheek and said, "You know, I could have killed you that day, I was so mad. Still, I should thank you. I mean, what would have happened if they'd left us up there?"

The three of us laughed and I got into my car. As I pulled away, I looked back at Jillie and her husband on their doorstep, arms raised in farewell. I thought I would remember them that way. But when I try, the details don't mesh. Each time, something more is missing—the shape of the house, or the tree I'm certain grew in front of it. Last time I forgot the sunglasses and I've changed the husband's hair several times and soon, I'm certain I won't see anything at all.

RESIDENT

Kugelmas is screaming about the engines again and I may have to kill him this time. "The politicos!" he shouts. "The engines of destruction!" he screams. He is on the table, waving his hands, making a racket. If I hadn't left the gun in 116, he'd be gone by now, Kugelmas the memory. I wheel over.

"Manny," I say. "Get down. You'll fall."

When he leans toward me, I see knees through his dressing gown. "The web of doom," he tells me. "They're constructing it on the roof."

Jake and Muhammad are there now, Jake with his armlock around Kugelmas's legs. Muhammad says to me, "It's okay, Isaac. Go back to the TV."

"Any word from Lillian?" I ask. "I wouldn't want to be late."

Muhammad shakes his head, no. Jake takes an arm off Kugelmas and points at the set. "It's okay," Muhammad says.

At the TV, Ada Fitz is all dressed up for the President.

Somebody told her he would be on *Jeopardy*. They are sweethearts, Ada and the President, and he calls her from the White House in the afternoons. They go out on dates every so often. He comes for her in his limo, late, when the orderlies sleep at the nurses' station. The President is on TV a lot these days, and Ada dresses up each time, the fur, the fancy hat, the cherries on the lapel.

"He's my sweet boy," Ada Fitz tells me.

On the television, a fat woman in a suit and a young black man play a game.

"That one?" I say. "The *schvartze?*"

"Scum," she tells me. "Jealous scum."

I mark Ada Fitz off for destruction, along with Kugelmas and Greenhouse the cougher. People are stacked along the walls here, the windows, in chairs, in walkers. Who knows what they look at? I head back to 116, where Lillian is probably annoyed over a burnt cheese sandwich.

When my Lillian died, she was fifty-four inches. The disease had eaten her up halfway already. In the box they put her and I said she'd roll, she was so small, she'd tumble and bruise herself. The man said there were pillows under her feet, soft pillows all around her. He was lying. I snuck in that night and there was Lillian, already with a bruise on each side of her face, and no pillows, not a single one. I got in with Lillian, there was plenty of room, and I held her, gently, gently, and when the earth turned, we tumbled, and I held her tight so she wouldn't hurt herself anymore. I was there two weeks. I would have stayed for good, I didn't care, but Nurse Samuels pulled me out. What's happening to Lillian now, I don't know, but I hold Nurse Samuels personally responsible. This I've got in writing.

On the way to 116, I stop in to see Letty. She is in her

chair by the window, very pretty. They've done her hair and she looks just like Norma Shearer. I tell her. The doctor, the one who won't tell me his name, said be sure not to bother Letty, she can't hear a word you say anyway. She can't understand if it's day or night, he said. Letty has made me promise to kill this doctor, and I would be happy to oblige, but I've killed one doctor already this month, and the elevator man, and I have to be careful not to arouse suspicion.

I push myself over to where she sits in the sun. I put my hand on hers, and we breathe in the smell of flowers. "Soon," I tell Letty. "I promise you, soon." Letty opens her eyes and begins to sing, an old one from the thirties, a crooner. She does a wonderful job.

"Letty," I say. "You haven't lost a bit of it."

"Of course," she tells me. "What would you do then?"

"You were one in a million," I say. "Eight curtain calls at the Sunnyside Arena. Nobody could take his eyes off you."

This is when Lillian calls, and I hurry. She doesn't like a late luncheon. But in the room she is happy because our boys are home. Jerry is in such a rush to see us, he still has on his professor's gown. He sits on the windowsill reading. Charlie is the same, always the same, in the T-shirt and long pants, beautiful, smiling like the sun. I know what it means to Lillian to have us all here. We sit down to a fine meal around the bed.

When Lillian begins to cry and Jerry turns his back, I wheel over.

"Don't cry," I tell her. "It's nothing. A bump on the head."

She turns away. Jerry and her hold hands, their backs toward me. "He bumped his head," I tell her. "It's nothing. Would I hurt my own boy?"

But they know. Jerry can't stop her crying and neither can

I. He leads her out of the room, looking at me over his shoulder. "I'll go with you," I call. "Wait, I'm coming." But they are out the door.

Across the hall, Greenhouse the cougher is at his tricks, and then I hear Kugelmas. I reach under my bed for the gun.

Kugelmas is in bed, his baseball cap crooked and his glasses off. They've got his hands tied down, which only makes my job easier.

"Maury!" Kugelmas yells. *"Maury!"* He looks at me. "My son Maury invented this place. You hear that? He *invented* it. He'll throw you all in the street! Mau-*ree*!"

I raise my gun as Jake and Muhammad break in the door. Too late. I've fired the shot. Kugelmas is a goner. He lays back on his pillows, a handsome man, you would have to admit, and so much happier now. It's all the thanks I need.

In 116, Jake lifts me into bed and Muhammad comes in with Nurse Samuels.

"Isaac," she says. "Another busy day."

"Is it time for dinner now?"

"Almost," she says. "See outside? Almost evening."

"I'm so tired," I tell her. "Exhausted. I may not want any dinner."

"We'll see, Isaac," Nurse Samuels says. "We'll see."

She takes my hand in her lap and holds it. Jake and Muhammad stand there even though nobody's invited them. She tells them to leave. "Close the door," she tells them, and they do. "See?" she says. "We're alone now." She sits with me and we look out the window, where the sun goes down and children wearing striped shirts gather in the trees to watch. We sit, not talking, waiting for the dark to come, and the quiet.

GLASS

E very night they broke glass and Wright Bellamy wanted
to hide.

A woman on the fifth floor began it. Wright could see her,
wild-haired, crazy, waving a coffee cup against the sky. "Who
do you think you are?" she screamed, every night, "Who do
you think you are?" and Wright had no idea whom she was
calling to. By the time she had thrown the cup hard on the
air-shaft pavement below, the others would have gathered in
their windows, bottles in hand, plates, mirrors. A black man
bit the end of light bulbs and lofted them like grenades; a
woman in a baseball cap sailed plates like Frisbees that arced
alarmingly close to Wright's building. They shouted, they
laughed, and Wright watched them, not knowing what to do.
When he looked over at Sharon, she smiled, and in her shrug,
in the flat upraised palms she offered, Wright saw none
of the emotions he was suffering, and that was the worst
feeling of all.

They had been roommates three weeks, and Wright considered Sharon and this apartment with the rapt tenseness of a dreamer afraid to waken. She was twenty-two, fourteen years his junior, and of a different generation entirely. She wore exercise clothing around the house, hats with veils and flowers, men's suits, army fatigues, and she looked born for all of them equally, in constant bloom. She dated college professors, rock guitarists, a utility infielder on the Mets. She might sleep till four in the afternoon, or be up at six, meditating in the early light. Everything she did surprised him. To Wright, she was of that breed of young women you saw everywhere nowadays, who carried loveliness and vigor with such remarkable ease, who seemed more comfortable in their young lives than he had ever been in his. To be living with her, sharing kitchen and bath, was a turn of events nothing short of miraculous. And this miracle had come about, Wright understood, from his finally taking matters in hand.

Wright's dream—it had always been his dream—was to build his own house. The board over his drafting table at work, the walls of the two rooms he rented from Mrs. Rosenblat in Flatbush, were covered with drawings, sketches, scaled and detailed blueprints of the houses he would someday build. For Cape Cod he had designed a two-story bungalow with a sun porch and a shed dormer for extra light. For Long Island he had drawn a Gothic Revival, all in wood, with church windows, a nave, transept, even a small rose window at one end. He had plans for redoing Victorians, landscaping the grounds of a Colonial, modifying a Federal house he had seen on a trip to Vermont. He had designs for a heating and cooling system that could run off solar power or wind; he had houses with live trees growing through them and streams running under glass floors; he drew rooms built onto solid bedrock and rooms opening onto chasms like the ones he imagined the Alps to overlook.

And then he had understood, in a moment of truth, that he would not build these houses. Wright believed in such moments; he paid close attention to eclipses, equinoxes, 11:11 each day and night: moments, he felt, of peculiar balance and revelation.

On his birthday, Bradley and two architects from the firm had bought him dinner, then taken him downtown to see a woman named Angel who could rotate her breasts in opposite directions while she danced. Bradley ordered Wright drinks he had never heard of and passed around a blue onyx bullet filled with cocaine. As birthday boy, Wright had the privilege of going onstage and receiving a kiss from Angel, but even with all the celebratory rounds in him, he had been timid, and Bradley got the kiss and applause instead. Bradley offered to get Angel's phone number, but Wright declined and went home, where he had been unable to sleep. He showered, tried to work on a drawing. He fed the landlady's cat, and still restless, showered again. He stood naked in front of the full-length mirror, while the cat, surprised by the untimely attention, mewled between his legs for more. Wright saw himself middle-aged, undeniably, with a belly gone slack and thinning hair. He saw the neat grooming, the hopeful shyness, the eagerness to please, even then, in the middle of the night, alone. He saw a nice guy, a thirty-six-year-old nice guy for whom time was not waiting.

In the morning, he had given Mrs. Rosenblat notice. He had sent a memo to Spencer, the architect he drew for, demanding a raise. At lunch he had gone to a singles' roommate service and talked to a young lady in an orange flattop who assured him she knew exactly what he needed.

He got the raise and found an apartment on Riverside Drive. A divorced bank teller in her fifties was the first to ask about the room, and after her a switchman for the Penn Central. When a grandmother with two cats and a schnauzer turned up one morning, Wright called the roommate service and told them he wouldn't need their help, but that afternoon, Sharon knocked at the door.

She wore a black dress under a red sweatshirt, a fedora and running shoes. Her long, brown hair was held back with large barrettes in the shape of paper clips. She carried a shopping bag full of peaches she had bought from an African on a blanket near the subway. He also sold incense, Sharon said, but she didn't have the cash. She stood in the hallway eating a peach. She offered Wright one. Wright took the bag from her and asked her to come in. She apologized for not calling, but she had been in the neighborhood looking for work and it seemed the easiest thing to do. Did Wright mind? The apartment was great, Sharon said. How long had he been living here? Was there a napkin she could borrow?

They sat on boxes and talked. She was from Colorado, originally, but had set out for New York as soon as she was able. She was looking for typing work now, but really had plans to design her own clothing and open a boutique. She had designed this outfit. What did Wright think? Wright told her he very much admired it. They talked over the rent, the utilities, but Wright would have given her the room immediately, without discussion. Giddy with the recent upheavals he had brought about, Wright watched her wrap the peach stone carefully in the napkin and knew he would not of his free will allow this woman to walk out of his life.

They carted his furniture from Brooklyn, her suitcase and rocking chair from Teaneck, where she had been living with an aunt. Wright bought rugs and claimed they were castoffs from Mrs. Rosenblat, paid for paint and tools and told Sharon they would work it out later. He built a new counter in the kitchen, a coat rack, a platform for Sharon's bed. He sanded floors and stripped woodwork. Sharon painted the kitchen carnation pink and put clouds on the blue ceiling over her bed so she would have something to look at in the mornings.

Everything seemed easy. Wright showed Sharon his case of drawings, afraid she would laugh. She loved them. She got thumbtacks and hung blueprints in the hall, over Wright's desk. She took one of the Victorians to hang in her room. Wright told her of his plans for the apartment, the lighting he would install, the bay window he had in mind for the living room. He told her he had wondered if he would have the opportunity to try any of his ideas. "I'm thirty-six," he said. "I wasn't sure I'd get the chance." And when they were done, with the plants hung and the carpets down and all the furniture in place, Sharon came home with a bottle of champagne. "It's perfect," she told Wright. "I don't see why we'd ever leave."

She cluttered the sink and medicine chest with bottles and tubes of lotion which Wright couldn't bring himself to complain about. She used his razors and shaving cream, and Wright made certain there would always be enough of each in the house. In the mornings, she came out to make coffee in a T-shirt only, and when she saw Wright hesitating on the threshold, too shy to come nearer, she laughed at him and went into his room for his robe.

Wright was in love with Sharon and he realized she knew it. It was not an untoward passion, did not leave him breathless or fumbling for words. They were pleased in their apartment together and Wright expected nothing. One night, after drinks at the university jazz club, she took him to her room and they made love. In the morning, Wright watched her sleep, careful not to make any noise. When the alarm sounded, she kissed him happily on the cheek and went to shower, and Wright understood that nothing had changed between them. They did not discuss it. He was home when she returned from dates, and if he heard a man with her, he would close the door to his room and pretend to be sleeping. If she were alone, they might share a bottle of wine or catch a late movie. Sharon told Wright he should get out more; she teased him about his habits, but Wright didn't mind. He felt they both knew how happy he was, and would have remained, if not for the glass.

They had heard sounds from the street, of course, voices, random city noises. One night a drunk on the corner had kept them awake singing the score to *Fiddler on the Roof*, and occasionally Wright thought he heard some commotion from the building across the air shaft. On the whole, though, it seemed a quiet street, lined with trees and makeshift gardens, as pleasant a street, Wright thought, as one could expect to find in New York.

The first time was the evening Wright made stir-fry shrimp. He was serving rice from a steaming wooden bowl when a woman shouted in the street, a horrible sound. They went to the window expecting to see an accident, an assault, but could see nothing. Then Wright spotted her on the top floor of the building opposite. She screamed again and threw something. She shook her fist and spat, and then, as Wright and Sharon watched, windows throughout the building opened. Glass began to fly, from all directions it seemed, people shouting as if the world had gone mad on some secret signal. A woman in a Yankees hat threw teacups. Two red-faced men in stocking caps tossed soda bottles. Some were full, and the men leaned out their window to see the bottles explode on the pavement below. The smaller of the two looked up and saw Wright and Sharon watching. He was wearing a lumber jacket, green and black squares, and his cap was pulled over his eyebrows. He waved. He nudged his companion and the two of them waved, exuberantly, like children.

"Do you believe this?" Sharon said, and she looked at Wright and laughed.

"Something must be wrong," Wright said, and he tried to laugh himself. "Don't you think?"

Sharon looked back out the window. The two men still waved, their excitement almost mechanical now, like two dolls in a toy-shop display. Sharon giggled. She raised a hand and waved back. Wright tried to keep a smile on, though he kept his hands firm in his pockets.

The episode lasted five minutes and was over as abruptly as it began. Wright slid a window open and stuck his head out. No police cars. Below, a cat picked its way among the rubble and broken glass. Somewhere a game show played on a television. No one else, as far as Wright could see, had been disturbed by the commotion.

Sharon was back at the table. "What was that all about?" she said.

Wright put his hand over the bowl of rice to test its heat. "I thought somebody had jumped from the roof," he said, "or the building was on fire."

"Maybe it was a celebration," Sharon said.

"A celebration? Of what?"

"I don't know." She held her chopsticks in the air as Wright doled shrimp onto her plate. "Like when they brought in the astronauts, remember? Or the hostages. Like that."

"Should we do something?" Wright said.

"What can we do?" Sharon said. "Let's eat."

They watched the eleven o'clock news but no mention of the incident was made. Wright wondered if the police had come and Sharon assured him someone must have called. After she had gone to bed, Wright stood awhile at the window. The building across the way was like any other, quiet, almost serene in the moonlight.

At work the following day, Wright checked every page of the *Post* and *Daily News* but could find mention of it in neither. He took it up with Bradley. Bradley was a student at NYU doing an internship with the firm. He was twenty-four or -five, wore expensive shirts, suspenders, seemed to have a limitless supply of pastel-colored shoes. He spent most of his time reading spy novels with his feet propped up on his drafting table. Wright was certain he would never last the semester, but Bradley seemed unconcerned.

"You'll never believe this one," Wright said, trying for a note of amusement. Bradley's book cover showed a syringe dripping blood. The blood pooled in the shape of a naked woman. He did not look up. "We were eating," Wright said, "you know, a romantic dinner for two? I've got the table set, the food's nearly on the plates, and there's this horrible scream. Like someone being attacked. Murdered, maybe. Right outside," Wright added, trying to get Bradley's attention.

"What did you make?" Bradley asked. He turned a page.

"Shrimp," Wright said. "Stir-fry shrimp with rice. Anyway, you can imagine what we thought. We go to the window expecting the worst, but we can't see a thing. Then the building across the way goes nuts. Screaming, throwing glass, absolutely nuts." Bradley looked up a moment. "Sharon was very upset," Wright said. "We both were. You hear about it on the news?"

Bradley put the book down on his knees. "Listen," he said. "Have you heard about this guy in Pelham? The subway executioner? This guy sneaks in the train shed every night and executes an IRT local. With a shotgun. Only the locals. The cops think a disgruntled employee, maybe, or a long-suffering commuter." He picked up his book. "I ride that train," Bradley said. "Now *that's* scary."

That evening was Sharon's turn. She'd gotten a recipe from one of Wright's books, and they were having a glass of wine, waiting for the clam sauce to simmer. Wright had put some Billie Holiday on the stereo, and Sharon didn't seem to mind. The wine went warmly to his head, and he was thinking of asking Sharon to dance, right there in the living room, when they heard the shout outside. Sharon rushed to the window.

"There she is," she said.

"Who do you think you are?" the woman screamed. "Son of a *bitch*!"

Wright joined Sharon and they witnessed the entire scene, exactly as it had been the previous evening. The woman shouted, leaning so far out her window, Wright was afraid she might fall. Two dogs had gotten into the air shaft somehow, and they barked at the building, dodging the falling glass. Somewhere in the din, Wright heard singing. The two men in the caps were there, and they noticed Wright and Sharon immediately. "Who do you think you are?" they called, waving. "Who do you think you are?"

Wright left the window to finish his wine. He shut off the stereo, switched on the television, went in to try the clam sauce. He added garlic without asking Sharon, tasted it again, and finally, when he could no longer stand it, went into his bedroom and phoned the police. Sharon was still at the window when he came out.

"They're coming," he told her. "The police are on the way."

The riot had died down but still the two men were there, arms flapping idiotically in front of grinning faces. Wright measured them with a look of pure hatred.

"Why do you stand there?" he said.

"They're so funny," Sharon said.

"Insane," Wright said. "That's insane, not funny."

"They won't stop," Sharon said, and there was no comfort for Wright in her laugh. "Should I wave back?"

"Let them wave at the police. They've got places they can wave the rest of their lives."

Sharon looked at Wright. Her expression was patient, slightly amused. The same expression, Wright thought, with which she had been looking at the two men. He didn't know what to say so he apologized.

"No," Sharon said. "You're upset. I apologize."

She turned down the television and sat by him on the sofa. "I'm sorry," Sharon said. "It's nothing to laugh at, is it?"

"No," Wright said. "It's nothing to laugh at," and he took hold of one of her hands, then let go. "We live here," he told her. "All this doesn't bother you?"

She looked at him, still smiling, he thought. Her hair was pulled back with blue and yellow clips that looked like clothespins. She adjusted a blue clip and put her hands in her lap. "Yes," she said. "It does."

Wright had more he wanted to say to her. He felt for a moment that he might do anything, say anything to her.

Instead, he went into the kitchen, where clam sauce was bubbling onto the stove.

Over the next two weeks, Wright phoned the police nightly. He did not believe such a thing could be allowed to continue. There were laws, after all, and there were taxes. What else were they for? But he did not seem able to make anyone at the station understand. Still he called, until he thought he could detect recognition, even annoyance, in the police operator's voice.

"Good evening, sir," she said. "What is the nature of your complaint?"

"Look," Wright said. "I know you're busy. I'm not a complainer, not usually. But this is right outside my window. How am I supposed to live with this?"

In the ensuing silence, Wright thought the operator was considering his question. He had gotten through. He envisioned himself going down to the station, after the whole thing was over, and thanking her personally. After thirty seconds she said, "Are you there, sir? What is the nature of your complaint?"

He continued calling, but as far as he could tell, the police never arrived.

At first, Wright refused to go to the window. He rearranged the furniture, upsetting the balance of his design, to face away from the offending wall. He was grateful when Sharon didn't object. She took him to an Italian place on Amsterdam one night, and another night, put the six o'clock news on so loud, Wright could feel it in his teeth. They ended up slumped over with laughter. Sharon had gotten work with a one-man law firm and was working late many evenings. Wright and she had dinner twice a week regularly, but he was alone in the apartment much of the time. He tried working on his drawings. He sketched in a fieldstone fireplace for Sharon's room, though there was no chimney there. He tried music to counteract the noise, Duke Ellington, Mozart, Vivaldi. Beauty over chaos, he thought, but the music was simply ruined. He tried Mahler then, for the volume, and was disgusted to find that Mahler complemented the tumult perfectly.

He tried going out. He went to early movies, and took Loretta, a friend of Bradley's, to dinner. But all he could talk about was Sharon and the glass, and before long the girl had gone strangely quiet and Wright realized she was embarrassed. He stayed in again, did his best to ignore it, to be cooking or vacuuming or on the phone when he thought he could feel the first scream gathering. He refused to allow himself near the window at first, but nothing worked, until, many evenings, he found himself sitting in the dark, his ears pricking at every sound in the street like a man frightened from sleep by an intruder.

Wright pulled back the curtains. Through the condensation of his breath on the glass, the building across the courtyard pulsed and refracted light. He checked his watch. He had begun timing them, but the lady on the top floor was erratic. Yesterday, Wright had watched the black man—the one who bit light bulbs and sang—push a half-size refrigerator through his window. The crash it made had been so tremendous that Wright had jumped backward, knocking a peperomia out of its hanger onto the floor. The refrigerator lay on its side now, hugely white and obscene in the clutter of glass, a cat perched on its sprung door.

Over Wright's bed, new drawings had appeared: mounds of

rubble rising above rooftops, bodies being tossed from windows, hands, fingers, eyes. He had not seen Sharon in three days. The other morning, when she came back to get a change of clothes, Wright had made a suggestion to her. A new apartment. On the East Side. They had them with views of the river. Expensive, of course, but he had money saved, and what good was it doing in the bank, after all. He'd spoken to a realtor. He could take off work, if she liked. If she wanted, they could start looking right away.

Sharon watched him over a pile of clothing she was taking to the cleaners. She looked ill, frowzy and unrested. She'd been staying at Gilbert's house most nights, but once or twice Wright had heard her arguing on the phone. She looked at him over the clothes and said, "Not now, Wright. Don't talk to me about this now."

He followed her into the foyer, halfway into the hall. "Will you think about it?" he called after her. "Will you let me know?"

At the elevator Sharon dropped the clothing into a heap at her feet. "I'm not moving, Wright," she said. "You do what the hell you want," and she walked to the staircase at the end of the hall, leaving the clothes, leaving Wright to come out in his pajamas and carry them inside.

She had called from work and apologized. It was Gilbert, she said, not Wright. It was a bad habit of hers taking it out on the wrong people. Gilbert had been asking—demanding might be more accurate—that she move in with him, and she had told him she'd think about it. That hadn't been enough for Gilbert. Anyway, that wasn't any of Wright's problem. Could she make him dinner? Could they just have a quiet evening together and talk?

She had gone directly into the kitchen when she arrived and

had been there nearly an hour, coming out only once, to ask what coriander was and if they had any in the house. She was just finished. The burritos were on the table, and Sharon, in a simple black dress with nothing in her hair but a tortoise-shell comb, was waiting for Wright to open the wine. Wright knew this. He checked his watch again when he heard Sharon pop the cork from the bottle. He was certain the lady would begin any moment. Once she did, it would be all right.

"I know I'm not the cook you are," Sharon said from the table, "but I really don't think they'll be that bad."

"Of course not," Wright said. "I'll be there in a minute."

"What's so fascinating?"

"Nothing."

Sharon poured wine into her glass and let out an exaggerated sigh. "A lady rushes home to make her roommate a deluxe Mexican meal. She dresses up special, just for him. She buys the wine. She even opens the wine and pours it."

Wright thought he detected movement in the fifth-floor window. He couldn't be sure, however; it might be the reflection of passing clouds.

"Wright," Sharon said. "What are you doing?" When he didn't answer she brought her hand down on the table with a sound that made him start. "Wright!" He turned to her. She was standing, her face flushed and tense as she leaned toward him. "What are you *doing*? I came home to see you, not to watch you hide behind the curtains."

Wright walked to the table. Once he was seated, Sharon sat as well. She began filling his glass with wine. She smiled.

"Why do you let it bother you?" she said. "There's nothing you can do about it."

"I wasn't hiding," Wright said.

Sharon paused. The neck of the wine bottle rested on the

lip of Wright's glass and threatened to topple it. Wright put a hand out to steady the glass. Sharon put the bottle down. "I'm sorry," she said.

"I wasn't hiding. I just didn't want your two friends to see me and start their act."

"My friends?"

"Those two men. The ones you find so amusing."

"They're not my friends, Wright."

"This is my living room, isn't it? Why would I need to hide in my own living room?"

He poured himself some wine and they ate in silence. The burritos were good. Wright wanted to compliment her but the words would not form. He had not meant to sound that way. Hurt. Peevish. He had important things to tell her, about the new apartment, about her clothing design idea. He had decided to help her, if she'd let him. But he would never get the words out if he sounded that way. You live here, too, he wanted to say. Why is this just my problem? He did not realize he had stopped eating until Sharon spoke.

"They're dried out," she said. "Don't eat them if you don't want to."

"No," Wright said. "I like them. You can taste the coriander."

Wright tried to eat with energy, but he could tell, from the way she glanced at him and did not speak, that she was upset. And the fact that she was, clearly, upset about him—upset *for* him—only added to his unease. She behaved as if he were overreacting, as if all this were simply moodiness. He feared her concern, and the possibility that she might have begun to pity him came at him like a rebuke, though she hadn't said a word.

Even across the room, he could hear the rumble of the

lady's window opening, but he didn't move. With the first surge of her shriek, Sharon gave him a quick smile. He acknowledged this, but when the other windows began slamming open and when the glass started to fall, Wright gave no indication he could hear anything at all. It would be over soon, and they would be okay. This was their first evening together in a week. It was early. He had a Nancy Wilson album he wanted to show Sharon. He would put it on the stereo and if it turned out she liked Nancy Wilson, this time he would ask her to dance. There was certain to be a movie on, and if she was not tired, they could sit up late and talk.

Wright continued eating, rigid with composure, and did not move even when a new sound pierced all the rest—not a shout or a howl, but a cry of real pain—and Sharon left the table. He heard her go to the window and he heard her say, "Oh, no," softly, and only when she called to him did he turn and join her.

The smaller of the two men held a bleeding hand behind a broken window. He and his companion, and across the way, Wright and Sharon, stood looking at the hand, and Wright could see blood streaking the forearm like veins, as if the order of everything had been reversed and the veins lay outside the skin. The tall man touched the wound lightly, and then looked up at Wright and Sharon. He waved slowly.

Feeling feverish, Wright raised the window. "You'd better get a doctor for that," he called out.

The men gave no response. The riot was in full swing and Wright could hardly hear himself above the din. He was afraid he would swoon, and put his head down.

"We've got to do something," Sharon said.

Across the courtyard, the taller man still waved, and then the man with the cut hand lifted it and began to wave also.

Wright raised his own hand then, not to wave, but to make them stop, to get their attention while he thought of what to do next. Sharon hit him hard below the ribs.

"He's hurt!" she said. "Can't you see that?" Wright stepped back. He was afraid she would hit him again. "You're laughing at them. Can't you see something's wrong?"

When Sharon looked back across the courtyard, the men had gone. She left Wright and went into her bedroom. He heard her phone the police and demand an ambulance. She called back twice in the next few minutes, the second time taking down the responding officer's name and badge number. He heard her arguing with Gilbert. "I don't want to talk, Gilbert," she said. She said, "I'm asking you for help," and hung up.

Wright waited for her. They could not leave it this way; surely, she'd give him a chance to explain.

When she closed the front door behind her, Wright rose to clear the table. He put the rice in an airtight container and wrapped the burritos in foil. He recorked the wine. He wiped off the table, cleaned the dishes and put them in their place in the cupboard. He pruned the damaged peperomia and wiped dust from the leaves of a dracaena. He sat in the half-darkness looking across the courtyard, where evening light played on the windows of the now silent apartments.

At the office, Bradley offered sympathy. He had just received an enthusiastic review from the partners, though Wright had not seen him work ten solid minutes the entire semester, and he claimed Wright's distress was his own. Wright hated revealing his private life to Bradley, but Bradley seemed to know women, Wright thought. At least he was always talking about them.

"You undervalue yourself," Bradley told him. "You sell yourself short. What is this, chicken?" They were at Wright's table, and Bradley was sampling the sandwich Wright had not touched. "This isn't chicken. They tell you it was chicken?"

"It's tuna," Wright said.

"It's not tuna. It's definitely not tuna. You gonna eat it?"

Wright did not respond and Bradley moved the sandwich closer to the filing cabinet where he sat on a pile of Wright's drawings. He spoke between bites.

"What's this girl's name? Shirley?"

"Sharon," Wright said.

"Shirley, Sharon. Fresh out of college, right? Homecoming queen, turtlenecks with little teddy bears, teeny pearl earrings. Am I right?" Wright shook his head, no, but Bradley wasn't watching. Bradley was finishing his junior year at college. That he managed to talk to Wright, and to everyone else, as if he were senior in experience to them all always irritated Wright, who listened grudgingly anyway. "Chicks that age, they don't have the complete emotional arsenal of a mature woman. Believe me. She wouldn't know she stepped in dog shit unless you told her." He paused over the sandwich, nearly gone now. "This is pretty good," he said. "I think it is chicken. Last bite?"

Wright shook his head and Bradley made a ball of the foil wrapper and tossed it, hook-shot fashion, over Wright. "Swish," Bradley said. He leaned closer. "Okay. I can tell this girl doesn't know anything. She's got absolutely no outlook. You, on the other hand, are a mature individual, highly respected in your field. See? What does she take you for, this Sheila? She shapes up or she's out on the street in her Dr. Denton's, *capisch*?"

"I couldn't tell her that."

"Why not? What's it to you some jerk got himself bloody? This is New York. With chicks you need an agenda."

"I could tell her I love her."

"Yeah, if you have to."

"I could tell her I was wrong."

"Good. Chicks love a guy with a conscience."

When Sharon opened the door, Wright was waiting. The table was set with the previous evening's meal. He had bought new candles and a fresh loaf of bread so they could start the meal again, exactly as they had meant to. Sharon walked by him, into the kitchen, where she rummaged in a drawer. She came into the living room with scissors, a roll of tape. She put these in her shoulder bag.

"I'm sorry about last night," she said.

"I am too. I wanted to tell you. I wanted—"

"I thought he was seriously hurt. It looks worse than it is. The main thing is to keep it clean and I'm worried he won't."

"You've seen it?"

"I took him to the hospital. I wasn't going to wait for the police. He needed a dozen stitches."

"I didn't hear you come back."

"I went over to Gilbert's."

She didn't say anything more and Wright waited for one of the speeches he had rehearsed to form in his brain. None did. He felt a rushing sensation, as if he had become aware of his blood's motion. He felt, also, distinct parts of himself, the back of his neck, his fingertips. He looked out the window. He could not let her leave again.

"Look," Sharon said. "I'm going to change the bandages. I could use your help."

"I made dinner."

"Louie, the one who cut himself, is the worse of the two. William's not much better, though. They've been in institutions most of their lives." She looked at him. "They're very friendly."

"Don't they have a doctor?"

"Of course they don't have a doctor, Wright. They're two disabled men living on welfare."

He thought of touching her, holding her here. "How can you go there?"

"Where?"

"That building. How can you go in there?"

She looked at him as if she were about to say something, but thought better of it. "You'd better stay here, then," she said, starting for the door.

The foyer of the building was dark and covered with litter. Graffiti was scrawled over the walls, and the inner, security door was off its hinges entirely, leaning against the jamb. There was hardly any light. Wright thought he should lead the way, was willing to, but Sharon did not wait for him. He followed her up to the third floor. This, too, was covered with trash, and Wright thought he could hear something rustling low against the wall. Sharon stopped before one of the doors and knocked. Someone touched the locks from inside, but did not speak. "Let's leave now," Wright said, quietly. "We can still go back." She ignored him.

"William?" she said. "It's Sharon. From yesterday. I came to see Louie's hand."

They stepped into a single room, bare except for a table, a mattress in one corner and a pile of bedding in another, two striped lawn chairs. Magazines and food wrappers were scattered on the floor, and what looked to be an entire side of bacon lay on the table, filling the air with the sweet odor of early rot. Louie, one hand in bandages, got up from the mattress. His face was broad and pliant, and he smiled. He raised the hand high and turned it to show Sharon he had kept it clean.

William closed the door behind Wright. "Hi," he said.

"This is my friend," Sharon said. "William, Louie, I want you to meet Wright Bellamy, a very nice man."

Louie approached with his good hand extended and Wright took it, briefly. It was damp and thick and Wright did not want to touch it long. William raised one of his hands and made a waving motion. Sharon laughed.

"That's right, William. The man in the window." Louie, glancing first at Sharon, began to laugh also, looking at Wright. "See?" Sharon said to Wright. "They know who you are. Okay, Louie. Let me see that hand."

Wright remained where he was as Sharon and Louie went to the table. William followed. She put her shoulder bag down and Wright thought she looked up at him, but he could not be certain. His eyes were not focusing. He had trouble getting his breath. Sharon switched on a light overhead and took Louie's hand in hers. "Do you want to help?" she asked William. She gave him a package of gauze. "Hold this for me, okay?" Louie brought his shoulders up and made a kissing sound at William, who let out a long thin giggle. Sharon's fingers moved expertly around the hand, nimble and assuring, and Wright wondered where she had learned to do such things. When the soiled bandages were removed, she cleaned the wound with antiseptic and Louie began to weep.

"Louie cry," William said.

"I know," Sharon said. "It hurts."

"Louie break window," William said, shaking his head. "Stupid Louie."

"It was an accident," Sharon said. "We'll get a new window and forget all about it. Wright, could you help me now?"

Wright approached the table. The smell here was stronger and he looked at the sagging brown and white ridges of the bacon. There were other smells in the air—urine, mold, something high and metallic that reminded him of hospitals. He breathed quickly, trying to keep the bad air from his lungs.

Sharon said, "He's lost one of the stitches. I need you to hold him while I clean it out."

Wright smiled to show he meant no harm, but in Louie's face he saw only uncomprehending fear. When Wright took hold of the hand, Louie pulled away sharply. Wright continued smiling and grasped the hand roughly, turning it to the light. Sutures crossed the palm in two hash marks, the flesh swollen and pink under the precise black thread. At the base of the thumb, a stitch had worked loose, and in the pucker between the edges of the wound, Wright could see dirt and inflammation. Sharon daubed the area with gauze.

"You've got to hold him better than that," she said.

Wright increased his pressure on the hand and felt the bones move underneath. Louie wept soundlessly.

"I'm sorry," Sharon said. "I know."

"Sorry, Louie," William said.

When she had cleaned the hand, she began wrapping it in gauze. Wright did not look up. It had grown silent enough in the room that he could hear the two men breathing, and through the broken window, sounds from the street.

"I need tape," Sharon said. "Three or four pieces. There's a scissors in my bag."

Wright cut three pieces from the roll. When Sharon asked

for a long strip, he put the scissors down to pull out the tape. William picked up the scissors. Wright paused, the tape in the air between them. He looked over at Sharon, but she was busy with Louie's hand. William moved toward Wright with the scissors and Wright shoved him hard in the chest. William staggered backward and the scissors fell to the floor. Wright grabbed them. He backed away, holding the scissors in front of him. William stood where he was, covering his chest with his hands. Louie licked his lips fast, looking from Wright to the floor. Sharon let go of his hand. For a long moment they all stared at Wright, who felt their eyes on him in the silence and did not dare approach.

"He took the scissors," Wright said, pleading. "It might not be safe."

Sharon looked at him, with contempt, as a stranger might. "Give them back," she said.

"What?"

"Give William the scissors."

Wright put the scissors on the table and went to the windows. He could not get the intact window to open, so he pulled newspaper out of the hole in the broken one. He tried to breathe slowly.

Behind him, he could hear Sharon speaking, not the words but the tone, soothing the two frightened men. She called his name, conciliatory, now.

Outside, the sun had dipped low in the sky so that his building, in shadow, seemed distant, removed. He located his own apartment easily, the drapes and back-lit plants unlike any others. He could see the coleus he had transplanted the other day, thriving, taut with vitality. The bird's-nest fern, also repotted, was doing well, so well it blocked sun from the aloe and grape ivy. He wondered how he had not noticed this before.

Sharon called to him again, but he did not answer. The sun had dipped further; shadow, pushing sunlight before it across the rubble in the courtyard, had reached the building where he stood. Wright checked his watch. From above him, he believed he could hear the first rasp of windows sliding open, the chime-like tingle of glass being gathered. Even the air seemed to alter, preparing itself.

"Wright?" Sharon was at his elbow. "I'm done. We can go."

He concentrated on the windows, searching out details. He could recite every item in the apartment, from the dishes in the sink to the precise angle of his slippers under the bed. Sharon touched him on the arm and this time he looked at her, but then looked away again.

"Wright," she said. "Let's go. We can go back now."

"No," he said. "We can't."

All around he heard sounds that signaled a readying—footsteps, voices, objects being dragged across the floor. Checking his watch would do no good; the lady on the fifth floor was often late. But she was always there to start it. It wouldn't be long. Sharon's hand was still on his arm and he put out his own to cover it. He looked at her and said, "Just one minute," and feeling the coolness of her skin under his, he turned back to the window and waited.

SOLACE

S unday mornings in winter, the boy waited for his father
to awaken. Lying in bed, with the room chilled around
him, he listened for the faint rumble of the water heater and
then his father's slippers on the hardwood floor. Outside his
window, the night shone blue as if cold reflected itself, and
stars turned over like falling ice.

He hurried into the bathroom when his father was done,
while the tiles still held warmth from the shower. The heater
was good for only one shower at a time, and the boy took his
in the evenings before the house cooled down. He pulled his
clothes on in the corner, his black tie, already knotted, already
in the collar of his white shirt. He brushed his teeth, splashed
his face, and pulled the tie close to hide a missing button.
When he opened the bathroom door, the smells from the
kitchen were in the hall: cocoa, cinnamon rolls, strong coffee.
The boy made his feet loud on the stairs so his father would
hear him coming, in case he had not yet mixed whiskey with
the coffee in his thermos. His father would be angry then.

He pushed the swinging door to the kitchen. His father sat at the table, straighter than any man he had ever seen, straw hat and newspaper before him on the immaculate white cloth. He had not heard. He held the big Stanley thermos in one hand, a bottle of Dewar's over the top with the other.

He said the boy's name: "Stuart."

The boy took a step back and watched the wooden door swing to a stop.

To reach the hospital after the patients' breakfast, they had to leave before dawn. The car door handle stung to the touch, and the vinyl seats radiated cold. While his father drove, Stuart pulled his jacket up and closed his eyes, the motion jarring him to full wakefulness.

Paterson's predawn streets had once held out to him an excitement he could almost taste. The men in their long coats were spies; the barreling trucks, filled with machine guns and jewels; the cars that sped by without lights, fleeing gutted and smoking bank vaults on the other side of town. But his father and he had been making these weekly trips into New York for three years. Stuart pulled his jacket around him, closed his eyes, and moved toward his side of the seat, into the air heater's intermittent blast. His father sipped coffee and hummed show tunes, spirituals, tunneling after the headlights into the thinning dark.

They timed it right; they reached the George Washington Bridge for sunrise. Mists came off the river and Washington Heights was outlined in brightness. The suspension cables flickered by, singing, and the main support, just tingeing silver, sloped upward out of sight. His father said, "Take a look at that, would you? My God, just take a look at that."

Stuart opened his eyes, took in the view, then turned

toward his father. His father had had several cups of his mixture; he was leaning forward as though about to stand. Pushing over the steering wheel so he could see it all, his father lifted his face to the light from the east.

The hospital Stuart's mother had died in was on Roosevelt Island, in the East River. Stuart was six when she died, and she had been ill all of his lifetime. There was a question of contagion, and not being a robust child, he was not allowed to see her often. That, at least, was the way he remembered it.

The first time was soon after she entered the hospital. Stuart remembered coming into the long ward and somehow, knowing which bed was hers, running directly to it. He remembered she looked very pretty and sad in her white gown, and that they had to leave because she was tired.

The other time was just before she died. Her skin was puffy like a baby's and there were wide bruises around her eyes as if she'd been hit. Tubes were running into her and she couldn't have moved her arms if she'd wanted. She opened her eyes at one point and looked directly at Stuart, but he didn't know what she saw. When they took him away from the bed, he didn't want to see her anymore.

The hospital walls were green, the color of shallow water. Stuart's father assumed he would keep up. He walked ahead, pants floppy on his thin legs, briefcase swinging. The Volunteer office did not open until 10 A.M., and they no longer bothered with it.

Men were lined up in the hallway, some in chairs, some prone on white-sheeted carts. The men were naked under their loose hospital gowns and some did not cover their thighs as Stuart and his father passed. His father nodded to a black man by the window who followed them with eyes and a face completely without expression.

They entered the ward, a long room with thirty beds on a side. Tables were arranged in the center aisle, and two men played checkers while a third leaned over the board. Music from a transistor radio echoed flatly along high walls which curved overhead into a wide archway, painted blue. Stuart's father stood by the entrance; he was handsome, with the strained, eager look of a man searching a gangplank for relatives. His eyes were active, his face worked elaborately around a smile. The hand holding the thermos shot into the air and Stuart followed his father to a bed on the far right.

Mr. Dobkin sat erect, white hair combed to a gentle crest across his scalp. His mild blue eyes caught light, and his expression was of small, perpetual surprise. A hollow tube projected from the middle of his throat, and through this, he breathed. He tried not to move his head.

"Mr. Dobkin," Stuart's father said. "You look wonderful."

Mr. Dobkin smiled. The bed was neatly made around him, his feet, two slopes halfway down the mattress. There were two chairs, one covered with clothing. On the cluttered nighttable was a black-and-white photograph of a young woman whose lips had been retouched bright red. Her lips made her look like she was waiting to be kissed. Stuart's father poured coffee into the thermos top.

"We came to see you first of all, Mr. Dobkin." His father spoke loudly, animatedly, and around the room, heads looked up. Some of them smiled. "In the car on the way over, Stuart said, he said, 'Daddy, why don't we go see Mr. Dobkin as soon as we arrive?' I believe you must be his favorite."

The boy looked at his father, then back at the man in the bed.

Mr. Dobkin raised a tissue to his throat. His voice was like a hull scraping rocks and came from somewhere in his chest. The boy could not understand what he said. His father laughed.

"Stuart? Of course. What did you think? Stuart, come say good morning to Mr. Dobkin."

Stuart tried to watch the blue eyes as he approached. On the blankets, a thin green tube coiled toward a machine behind the bed. The old man smiled. His hands felt smooth on the boy's skin, dry and fine like worked wood. They moved up the boy's arms until the elbows, where they gripped and gave him a little shake. His father laughed again. Mr. Dobkin turned his head carefully a few degrees and groped around the nighttable. He brought back a round tin with a painting of a girl sitting among sheep on its cover. With delicate fingers, he twisted the lid off and held the tin out to the boy. Small crescent-shaped candies lay in a dust of sugar powder. Stuart took a candy and felt its weight on his tongue.

"You spoil the boy, Mr. Dobkin." His father's voice was rich with pleasure. "You'll spoil him silly." He raised the briefcase onto the bed and sprang the snaps. "Well. What will we have today? Epic? Romance? Milton?" His bright eyes ranged the wall above the bed. "Or more from Lord Alfred, yes, Mr. Dobkin?

> Now folds the lily all her sweetness up
> And slips into the bosom of the lake
> So fold thyself, my dearest, thou, and slip
> Into my bosom and be lost in me."

Stuart sat in the chair which was draped with the old man's clothing. He held the book on his knees and read the poetry with his eyes to the page, and he did not stop, even when Mr.

Dobkin pulled the green tube to his throat and the suction machine clattered to life.

They stopped at most of the beds in the ward, then at many in the identical ward on the floor above. Stuart's father had something for every patient. He knew which ones to soothe, which to joke with. He remembered that Mrs. Dorsey's grandson was a running back on his high school team, and that Mr. Feld was inconsolable over the loss of a set of dental plates. He sat by the beds and talked about whatever they wanted. He sipped his coffee and nodded his head, and when a man with pneumonia asked to have some letters mailed, he sent Stuart to the mailbox in the lobby immediately, so they would be in the early morning pickup.

When Stuart returned, his father was sitting by the bed of a man with a beard who was wiping his eyes. "This is my boy, my son, Stuart. Wordsworth is his favorite poet, too," his father said.

Stuart held the worn poetry book, the texture of the leather coming through to his fingers. He read "My Heart Leaps Up" and a section of *The Prelude* his father chose. When he had finished reading, he waited. The two men looked into the air in front of them.

In the cafeteria, a young black man with an athlete's body lay his head on the table and pushed food into his mouth with a hand. When he lifted his head, there was food on his face and his eyes were closed.

Stuart's father did not eat. He bought coffee and joked with the people behind the counter. They all knew him. The woman at the cash register gave him an apple and waved at Stuart. His father took his thermos and briefcase and left the room for a minute, and when he returned, added from the thermos to the coffee in his cup.

"How's the burger?"

"Okay."

"When I was your age, I could eat a ton of burgers. Six, seven, ten burgers. They had to pull me away from the table."

Stuart took a bite to indicate he could eat another hamburger if he had to. His father held out the apple.

"Mrs. Wilson said this is for you if you've been good."

Stuart took the apple. His father leaned forward and jabbed the air over his plate with a forefinger.

"I said, Mrs. Wilson, that boy's not just good. He's lucky. And I don't mean sweepstakes lucky, I don't believe in sweepstakes luck. Luck is just rewards, I said. Rewards to the deserving. That boy, I said, is a laborer. That boy knows about pain."

He brought his hand down to the coffee and raised the cup over his face. He nodded while he drank, sloshing coffee onto the lapel of his suit. He did not wipe it off.

"Look around this room, Stuart. There's your luck. These people need what we have to give. They *need* it. You know what's out there?" Without turning, he gestured at the window. "You know? Nothing. Cold, unforgiving nothing. You be glad we're in here, with work to do. You be glad."

A man in a wheelchair was having trouble maneuvering between the tables. Stuart's father took a quick swallow from his cup and jumped up to assist. Leaning over, with his mouth to the man's ear so they could talk, he pushed the wheelchair out the door toward the elevators.

Stuart put the apple down. Mrs. Wilson smiled at him and he looked away. Outside the window, asphalt stretched down to the river wall. A boy in a denim cap was throwing rocks at beer bottles he had lined up on the wall. When he shattered one, he performed a little dance of congratulation, patting himself on the back and waving his arms in the air. Beyond him, the muscular river coiled in the light. Stuart's father returned and sat heavily in his chair.

"Ezra Williams," he said. "Cancer. Five East. Remember cowboy books, Stuart. Zane Grey."

He looked at the floor and did not speak. Stuart looked out the window, pleased to see the boy had broken his last bottle. Throwing his remaining stones randomly into the water, he skipped onto the river wall and ran out of sight.

"Will we be leaving after lunch, Dad?"

"No. Too much to do. There's Lyle Johnson on three and that Russian woman in the thoracic unit. And Mrs. Holbrook. We've missed her two weeks now."

He began rummaging inside his briefcase. Stuart's face had grown hot and he could hear the river. He dropped the hamburger on the plate and pushed it away.

"What's the matter?" his father said.

"I don't want it."

"You have to eat, Stuart. A sound body is—"

"You didn't."

His father looked up from his briefcase, his mouth turned into a smile. "You don't want it?" His voice was very soft. "You don't? Then don't eat it, Stuart. Don't touch it."

"I had enough," the boy said, looking away.

"You had enough."

Stuart left the trays on the aluminum cart in the corner and followed his father into the bathroom. His father turned on the faucet, straightened the boy's tie, and ran a wet comb through his hair. Stuart felt the water collect in his shirt.

*   *   *

Mrs. Holbrook's bed was high off the ground and she lay beneath the blankets, massive and rising into the air. Something in her disease made her swell, and Stuart had seen four orderlies move her, each lifting a part, and once a tube had snapped, trailing liquid across the sheets. He stood by the foot of the bed and felt his breath escape in tiny spurts. He could hear the river, and he looked at the corners of the room and at the wide automatic doors leading out to the hall.

His father held her hands. Her fingers were gray and pliant, and the boy watched his father caress them. He patted and soothed; his hands said he would stay with her, he would not leave, and they did not stop, even when no words were being spoken.

"Mrs. Holbrook," he said. "We can't have that. We mustn't give in to despair. Sometimes I think despair is the only death, Mrs. Holbrook."

"My Anna stopped coming. I ain't seen the babies in weeks, now. One of them had a birthday in April."

"Anna must have her reasons. You know she must have good reasons."

"She don't come at all, now. I think the doctors told her she can get something from me and give it to the babies. She's afraid to come."

She was crying. She brought her eyes around; they were wild and white and her skin was gray. When the eyes passed over Stuart, his scalp tightened and the wind flew out of him. He inhaled deeply. The smell rising off the bed hit him with every breath, and every breath was a crashing in his ears.

"Anna loves you, Mrs. Holbrook," his father said. "This is hard for her, too."

The woman in the bed nodded and tried to smile. She looked again at Stuart.

"Would you like to say hello to Stuart, now? He's been anxious to see you all day. Would you like to say hello?"

Stuart walked to the side of the bed. The woman reached out and he leaned at the shoulders. Her hands touched his arms, his neck. She pulled him gently to her broad thawing chest and held him, stroking his hair. The boy was rigid, trying to be soft. In the chair, his father smiled.

When the coughs came, Stuart closed his eyes and tried not to hear. The coughs were deep and luxurious and tore easily through something in the woman's body. They came up in her chest to where the boy lay pressed, but her hand on his face continued, soothing, calm. He told himself to wait.

Stuart waited in the car, his father's thermos on his knees. The thermos was a cool blue metal that felt good to hold. It was a deluxe two-quart model, ordered directly from the company in Nashville, Tennessee. Stuart remembered the day it had come in the mail. His father had pulled it out of the newspaper wrapping and showed him the inside, the dark glass reflecting. More money than he could easily justify, his father had said with a smile.

Stuart slid off the front seat. Kneeling under the dashboard, he took the thermos in both hands and brought it down hard on the floor, over and over, until he felt something give way inside it. He leaned it against his father's door and sat back on the seat.

His father came across the lot to the car, briefcase swinging before him at every stride. When he opened the car door, the thermos fell to the ground and rolled, making a noise. His father put the briefcase down and gave Stuart a quick glance. The boy couldn't tell what was on his face. His father picked up the thermos, unscrewed the top, and poured. Through the brown liquid, shards glinted like bits of ice in his hand.

No word for
Mercy

The hospital's namesake, Ursula, led eleven thousand virgins to their drownings in the Rhine rather than see them debauched by a group of Huns in the vicinity. This was in the fifth century, near Cologne, Germany. Some say it wasn't drowning, but murder. Others claim there were eleven girls, not eleven thousand. Nina doesn't care. She says Ursula is the patron saint of virgins and fools who should have known better than to listen. This makes St. Ursula's the place for her, Nina says, because she was one until she married Lou, and has been the other ever since.

When I tell Nina I love her, she feeds me psychology textbooks, tracts on delayed adolescence. I return them with notes attached, buried in flowers, wrapped in brochures advertising weekends at the Lamplighter Inn, Marblehead. When Lou can't pick her up from her Philosophy of Language class Mondays and Wednesdays, I am there on Huntington Avenue, in the snow or the rain, waiting to escort her to the bus. We walk through the city holding hands while she lectures me on Wittgenstein and the possibility of communication. I nod a lot, ask appropriate questions, hold her hand until she's on the second step, halfway inside the bus with people watching. The night she and Lou come to the Dresden Cafe to hear my band, Grim Sewage, we shock the crowd by doing a slow version of "How High the Moon," Nina's favorite. Nina and Lou get up to dance, and by the end they're jostling kids with dog collars on, studs through their cheeks, live ferrets napping on their shoulders. Some of these kids are slow-dancing for the first time in their lives. They like it. The house gives us a standing O.

It has to end, Nina tells me. It will never work. She pshaws my love. You can't know love, Nina says, until thirty-five, when your hormones learn some manners. She says Plato says so. What do we have in common except overactive imaginations and an affinity for warm dark places? This is the way she talks.

It will work, I tell her, if she gives it a chance. It's got to.

Here in emergency, there are four of us: Gary, the night nurse, who in 1970 went behind the lines into Laos and is still making the return trip; Ernie, the ex-bank guard who was smoking in the can while robbers borrowed his Mercury Lynx to make a clean getaway; Nina, who greets the customers and answers the phone, and who, when the mood strikes, meets me behind the supply stacks in Radiology for some fervent, hurried love; and me, Clifford Dante Eastman (the first after my paternal grandfather, a furrier, the second after my mother's doctoral thesis), twenty-five years old, part-time musician and lapsed health food fanatic, nurse's aid. I am working the graveyard shift at St. Ursula's while I weigh my options.

*   *   *

Let me tell you about myself.

At Miss Harbison's experimental school, we were given paintbrushes instead of pencils and encouraged to sing first, read later. We were taught about government by the people early, and when we voted to cancel school for two weeks, our teacher—we called her Shelly—had no choice but to comply, and when we voted to execute Sidney Castle by hanging, on grounds of his general unpopularity, Shelly had to go to Miss Harbison for guidance. Several of my classmates have gone on to become geniuses. Several have not.

At Stevens Academy in Vermont, I began having dreams in which elderly people would sit at the foot of my bed and nudge me until I woke. They wouldn't speak, and we would sit there, sometimes until morning. The doctors told my parents this was night terror, and nothing to be concerned over, which made my parents glad, as they had troubles of their own.

At college I tried on several religions, majored in Post-Modernism, and in a series of Psych experiments, sat in a dark room and followed orders sent from pigeons in another dark room across the hall. I graduated with honors, prepared for nothing. I play bass in a punk-anti-nuke-blues band. Like many people, I try not to read the papers. My parents have dispersed. Mother left Dante and is CEO of a Fortune 500 investment firm, and Father is a parapsychologist with offices in Mexico City and Detroit. We see each other on designated family holidays. I am in love with Nina, a thirty-eight-year-old TV repairman's wife with two kids and designs on half a dozen master's degrees. My analyst, Bob, throwing his hands up, asked me one afternoon what I was so afraid of. In a fit of honesty I answered, "Whad'ya got?"

*   *   *

It is a Tuesday morning, past midnight, late October. We are in the basement of St. Ursula's, a small hospital toward the outskirts of Boston. High on Blake Hill, flanked on all sides by hospitals with national reputations and bustling staffs, we get a limited portion of Boston's accumulated misery and trauma. We do what we can. Above us—three floors, sixty-seven beds—sleep patients who were sent here because they needed a rest, or because rest was the only thing left to offer them.

Gary is watching *Wanted: Dead or Alive* on the TV. The TV is a small black-and-white, and Gary cradles it in his lap like an adored child. I've got exam rooms to clean, and a migraine customer sleeping off a Demerol swoon in room four. Still I sit, peering over Gary's shoulder at a young, smirking Steve McQueen. We've seen this episode eight times, by my count. Right now, Steve McQueen is demonstrating to a young boy named Luke the proper way to handle a gun. "That's it, gentle-like," I say, and then Steve McQueen says it.

Once Luke has perfected his gunmanship—over the course of a commercial break—he and Steve McQueen will be able to set out after the villains who killed his father and stole his horse.

Luke is like any good kid on the Hollywood range: he defers to his elders, is more concerned with recovering Dexter than with punishing his abductors, and, though he lives alone in a farmhouse half burned to the ground by the marauders, eating nothing, as far as we can see, he appears in each scene cheerful and bright, with groomed hair and a clean shirt. On the back lot where they practice shooting at a painted cactus, he calls Steve McQueen, "Sir."

"I think I'm getting the hang of it, Sir," Luke says.

I say, "I reckon you might be, little pardner," and Gary gives me a look.

The phone rings and Nina announces Mr. Friedman. "It's urgent, he says to tell you."

"Mankowitz again?"

"It would appear so," Nina says.

"Any mention of Phoenix?" I ask.

"None, Clifford," Nina says. "And I haven't inquired."

I cradle the receiver on my shoulder and twist away from Gary, speaking into the cleft between the meds cabinet and the wall. "Nina," I whisper. "Hey, Nina." Behind me come six rapid gunshots, then Steve McQueen's confident drawl: "That's good shootin', son." Luke says, "Thanks a lot, Sir." Nina says, "Save your breath, Cliffie. I've got home-work."

She prods me toward Law School, the Peace Corps, toward Maria, the new technician in the blood bank. Take a chance, Nina tells me. Get acquainted with your life. Through interhospital mail she sends me cautionary notes about stunted development, whole paragraphs from Karen Horney, the Freuds, father and daughter, William James. I counter with all the Marx I remember: " 'From each according to his ability, to each according to his needs.' P.S. Let me buy you lunch."

I meet Mr. Friedman in room three. Ernie, who is supposed to wait with the customers until I come out, is nowhere in sight.

Mr. Friedman sits in a chair, straw hat on his knees, beaming triumph up at me. He is dressed for the beach out at Wonderland: plaid shirt, khakis cinched high into pleats on his belly, canvas-topped shoes. For thirty years he laid road for the city of Boston; now he lives at the Somerset Hotel up the street and has dreams of persecution. I sympathize. He and Mankowitz, his roommate, are supposed to retire to Phoenix and learn how to play golf, but Mr. Friedman is having second thoughts. He's lived in Boston all his life. He's not quite ready to leave. Now Mankowitz, to move things along, has turned saboteur. The electricity has been tampered with, Mr. Friedman says, and his shaving mug, the one with Bobby Doerr on the front, has disappeared under mysterious circumstances. Several of Mr. Friedman's important documents have been replaced with papers he has never laid eyes on in his life. Why Mankowitz would do these things, Mr. Friedman doesn't know. The two friends haven't spoken in weeks.

Mr. Friedman smiles, gives me a salute, lifts a hand to show me what's inside. At first, I think he's found a dead bird, a baby. It lies pink and featherless in his palm. Then I see it's his hearing aid, curled into its flesh-colored earpiece.

"See?" he bellows.

I nod.

"Red-handed, we got him," he screams. "He thought I was sleeping, the son of a bitch." Next door, Gary pounds on the wall, but Mr. Friedman hears only his story. "I made like a dead man," he says, and shows me, head on one shoulder, mouth open, eyes closed. "You should be proud." I nod again, proud. "When he went back to his room, I found this in my head. Who knows what it is? I came right over."

I take the hearing aid from him and examine it. I spread sterile gauze on the instrument tray and place the hearing aid on top. With my little plastic ruler, I measure its height and width. Mr. Friedman watches with great interest. I get his vital signs. His blood pressure is 120 over 80, his temperature

98.6, exactly. He should live, here or in Phoenix, twenty more years.

Gary will be right in, I tell him. I hold the hearing aid square in my palm so he'll know I'm being careful with the evidence. "You know Scandinavian?" he asks. I shake my head, no. He shakes his head back at me. "Someone keeps talking Scandinavian."

While Gary is with Mr. Friedman, I am to watch the rest of the show and prepare a detailed summary. From the on-call room, Dr. Shepard shuffles in, scratching his head and wincing in all directions. He is wearing scrubs from another hospital and slippers of different colors. He sits next to me without saying a word and looks around for stray food items.

On the screen, two men lie facedown in the dirt, and Steve McQueen holds his shoulder as if he's been shot, but there is no blood. Luke hollers and runs to his horse. Dr. Shepard says, "We've seen this before, haven't we? I think I've seen this one." We've seen them all before. After the commercial, they are back at the farm, which is rebuilt. Luke asks Steve McQueen one more time if he won't stay. Steve McQueen just smiles and trains blue eyes on the horizon.

Steve McQueen rides off, attended by chickens and barking dogs, and the camera pulls in on Luke. The boy will be all right. We know it. He waves, using his cowboy hat, and we know he's gotten more than his pride back, his horse Dexter. Somehow in the last thirty minutes he's been given a home truth, a gift, something he will live by the rest of his life. We see his future in his face.

Gary comes in as the credits begin rolling. "You missed it," Dr. Shepard says, feeling with ten toes for his slippers. "They killed Steve McQueen. All of Whiskey Gulch is in mourning."

Gary ignores him. He sits in his chair and lights a cigarette. He leans back and puts his feet on the desk, his hands behind his head in a listening posture. He looks at me. "Okay," he says. "Tell me."

In the paper—somebody left it next to me on the bus—it said authorities are concerned about a new strain of rats near the waterfront. Apparently, these rats are ambushing tourists. A lady from Iowa City was chased by one swarm, only to find another waiting for her in an alley. She got several bites, refused treatment, and flew back to the Midwest. A prominent vermin expert decried the incident and two others as products of hysteria (human) and limited food supply (rat). He called reports of a Super-rat laughable. They may have the numbers, the expert said, but we have evolution on our side.

Myself, I wouldn't bet heavily against the numbers.

Near 3 A.M., Nina relents, agrees to meet me in Radiology. I've got news, I tell her, something important. Forget news, she says. Bertrand Russell's splitting her head wide open and she needs to lie down.

We've had no customers since Mr. Friedman, and only two calls: a mother wanting someone to talk with since her colicky baby was keeping her up anyway, and a gentleman who had heard that if you boil antifreeze with vinegar you get corn oil and wanted to know if we had the same information.

I leave Gary in the middle of *Hawaii Five-O*. After that it's *Star Trek* and *Alias: Smith and Jones*, so he won't be much for conversation in any case.

"Okay if I take a break?" I ask him.

"Look out, McGarrett!" Gary says. "Don't get in that car!"

On the floor behind the supply stacks is our spot, and we

use the heavy lead-lined mats they lay over the patients for our bed. I've mentioned to Nina that these are used to absorb radiation the patients need protection from, but she said lead deflects, doesn't absorb the stuff, and brought in two articles from *American Radiologist* to back her up. On the lowest shelf, behind a box of surgical masks furred over with dust, Nina keeps two diaphragm cases, one for her diaphragm and the other for her rolling papers and pot. I've mentioned, too, the No Smoking signs, but Nina just threatened me with more articles.

We lie together when we are finished, the chill of the room returning to our skins. I'd rather leave my clothes on the whole time, but Nina says if she wanted to fuck my clothing she'd visit my closet. She lights another joint and lies back, an open diaphragm case between her breasts for the ashes.

"Mitch says it's okay," I tell her, referring to my roommate, the drummer in Sewage. "His uncle will be gone two weeks. We can have the place anytime we like." She offers me the joint but I don't take it. "It's five minutes to the beach. Fishermen come up in rowboats and sell you lobster right out of the traps. There's a full wine closet, and a fireplace in the bedroom. There's a pond where Canada geese have babies. I told Mitch you're a great fan of Canada geese."

"I can't, Cliff," Nina says.

"Next week?"

"Either week. Lou's cousin is coming in from Portland, and next Saturday there's a PTA lunch at the school."

"Can't Lou go?"

"Lou is going, Cliff. We're going together."

"How about Sunday? We could drive down early, find those fishermen—"

"Cliff." She puts a hand on my lips. "I told you. I can't."

She kisses my mouth and my chest. She collects the diaphragm cases and hides them on the shelf. She slips into her bra and turns her back, lifting her hair so I can do the clasps.

"How's your reading?" I ask her.

"This guy asked Bertrand Russell if he believed in God," Nina says, buttoning her shirt. "The old man told him, 'I have no need of that hypothesis at the present time.' "

The foundation must be going. In room five, right next to the EKG monitor, a column of ants as wide as my arm is crawling up the wall. They start under the floor and end behind a ceiling tile. They move in both directions, in a lazy S. When I hold a box of Ace Bandages in their path, they accommodate me, sidling to the right. I turn out the light, close the door. Through the small glass window, I can still see motion on the wall.

After Erasmus, her second kid, was born, Nina decided to make some changes. She looked around and reasoned anything was possible. First came Anthropology classes: "The Sociology of Primitive Man" and "Fighter vs. Forager: A Dilemma Considered." Then the Psych courses: "Eros: Tyrant or Truant?" and "Human Love: A Dilemma Considered." Halfway toward degrees in each she switched to Philosophy: "Rationality in Reflux" and "Knowledge: Dreamstate or Dilemma?" She is five-three and blond. She combs her hair down her back or over one shoulder, depending on her mood. In a front tooth she has a calcium deposit shaped like an elephant, and her hands are delicate and small, even for someone her size. She has live blue eyes that could console me for anything. When she married Lou, she was young, too young, and though I assume he's a nice man with qualities of

92

his own, he cannot possibly love her the way I do. It's this I'm trying to tell her.

She explains to me about the language philosophers. We get in trouble, Nina says, by trying to say too much. We talk about ethics or metaphysics, about love, when we can't. All we have are facts, and facts are all we can talk about. She thinks I could learn from this, me with my butt on the fence waiting for the big answer, for God's starting gun.

At home, one of Mitch's girls is remodeling the living room. Her name is Chloe. She is near six feet, black, and I've never seen her before. They met at the Save the Seal rally, she tells me. Her T-shirt says, "Nuke Reagan." She's going at the wall between Mitch's room and this one with a sledge-hammer. She's making good progress. She asks me if I know anything about wiring, tells me there's coffee in the kitchen but it might be a little dusty by now.

On the table is my mail, all brochures: three for graduate schools overseas, a vocational training program in Florida, a six-month program to be a fire watcher in the Sierra Nevada. A fold-out brochure covered in dollar signs tells me I can earn big money making cannoli in my own home. I put them with the others in the box under the sink.

I make the mistake of listening to the radio. Half of Mattapan has burned to the ground. Eight communities are suing the state over toxic waste disposal, and one group is busing a load of children dying of cancer to the governor's office downtown. Scientists in New Zealand believe a change in the magnetic field may reverse the direction of plate tectonics, hurtling our continents into a heap near Paraguay.

When I try to sleep, Chloe sticks her head in and asks if the pounding is bothering me. I tell her no. I call Nina at home, though I've promised not to, and Lou, back for lunch, answers the phone. He says hello three times, and when I don't say anything, he tells me he's sorry, he can't hear me and would I please call back. He waits, and I can hear him breathing into the mouthpiece. I hang up. I call Bob, but his answering machine tells me he's out of town for the week. At the end of the message, I hear, "And if this is you, Cliff, take it easy, for God's sake. Get some sleep. Learn a mantra. Just try to relax."

In Harvard Square a woman holds a sign that reads, "You can't hug your children with nuclear arms." I walk over and ask her what it's supposed to mean and she gives me the finger. A bum walks up and asks for some change. I give him ten dollars and he runs off, looking at me over his shoulder as if I'm the one sleeping in my urine at the bus station. I sit in the park and drink coffee, decaffeinated. When I look up, the people in front of me are walking faster and faster until all of them are running. I don't want to know why. I head early for the hospital, where I might borrow Dr. Shepard's bed if he's not in it.

One theory about the earth's destruction is called Nemesis. According to this theory, our sun has a twin, Nemesis, which returns for a visit every twenty-six million years or so. When it passes through our galaxy, it creates all sorts of havoc, spraying comets around like a Roman candle. Last time it wiped out the dinosaurs. Scientists disagree about where Nemesis is in its orbit, but some time—if it hasn't already—it will make that final arc and head home, picking up speed along the way. Gary doesn't understand why I think about this. I don't understand how he thinks about anything else.

*   *   *

In Radiology, red lights blink serially along one wall, and there's a green light that glows brighter, or seems to, the longer you are in the dark. The air smells of ozone and feels heavy, depleted. Every few minutes, a machine switches on with a deep hum, drawing electricity and oxygen, nourishing itself through the night.

Nina told me the pot would help but she was wrong. My head is spinning. I lay back and listen to her voice, feel the throb of the machines in the floor under me. When the perimeter of my vision ribs with motion, I close my eyes. She hears my breathing alter and rubs my arm.

"You all right?" she says. I don't answer. She kisses my face and rolls on top of me, her breasts on my chest, her knees pressing my legs. She lets her hair fall to cover my eyes. "Clifford," she says. "Cliff. It's okay."

In my latest dream, the beginnings are different. I am asleep, or riding the T. I am making dinner in my kitchen at home or eating at a coffee shop downtown. I am in the reading room at the Public Library, under the portraits of the founders, by the sunny windows overlooking the courtyard. It doesn't matter where I am, because the next minute I am a thousand miles in space, the earth receding from sight so fast I don't have time to scream before everything goes white.

Nina knows what to do. She presses her body on mine. She holds me down for all she's worth.

"It's all right," she says. "I've got one for you." She puts her lips to my ear, whispers. "The Hoover Dam rises 726 feet above bedrock. It is concrete, forty-five feet thick at its crest, sixty-six feet at its base. The dam is 1,224 feet long. It is capable of storing 28.5 million acre-feet of water behind it. Listening? The dam contains three and a quarter million cubic yards of concrete. It weighs over six and a half million tons.

An earthquake of eight, of nine, wouldn't touch it, engineers tell us. It will be standing in ten thousand years."

When Nina finishes, she starts at the beginning, whispering into my ear, comforting me with data. She tells me about the Brooklyn Bridge, the Hancock Tower, Great Salt Lake. "Breathe," she tells me. She coaxes my lips with hers, brings my arms up to hold her. "You're all right," she says. "You're not going anywhere."

At the bus stop, a boy in a blue suit hands me a bumper sticker. It is blue and white with a dove to one side and it says, "Expect a miracle."

I trace Bob to Martha's Vineyard. Our connection is very bad. A woman keeps breaking in on the line, saying she can't hear Anita. Bob tells me the boy at the bus stop sounds dangerous and to stay away from him. I tell him my plan about Nina and he tells me she isn't the answer. "You're looking for her to give you permission to start your life," Bob says, shouting over Anita, who's come on the line. "She's got a life, Clifford," Bob says. "What do you have?"

We do two sets at the Dresden. During our jam on "Americium Blues," Chloe comes up onstage and starts screaming at Mitch. He can't hear a word she says. She grabs one of his drumsticks and throws it into the crowd. Nobody notices. She kicks over his tom-tom and stamps off. She's wearing my jacket and is carrying my leather stenciled suitcase. Later, Nina and Lou come in. They sit at a table to the side, and Lou goes up to buy drinks. We segue into "How High the Moon," and the kids start cheering. It's become our signature piece. I transmit all manner of telepathic signals at Nina. Wait. I need to talk. Don't go. I love you. They finish their drinks and head for the door. Nina waves and then Lou waves and points at his watch and shrugs and they're gone.

On Monday, Dr. Shepard tells me I look worse than a first-year resident. I've been having a little trouble sleeping, I tell him. He says he knows what I mean. Have I thought about medical school, he wants to know. I'd fit right in. I'm considering medical school, I tell him. It's definitely on my list.

At the bus stop, the boy in the suit is reading a bible. I tap him on the shoulder and give him a Grim Sewage T-shirt. It shows a smile face with just one dot in the middle and the smile. It says, "Mutants for nuclear energy." He thanks me and goes back to his reading.

Tuesday night, Mr. Friedman comes in complaining of stomach pain. Mankowitz is with him, helping him walk, though they still aren't speaking. Mankowitz is as thin as Mr. Friedman is stocky. He wears a worn brown suit and tie, and as he leads Mr. Friedman in, he looks worried. Mr. Friedman is still in khakis and beach shoes. "You think I don't know where this pain is from?" he says to me. "You tell him poison won't do it. I'll move when I'm good and ready." "Nothing more pitiful than a crazy old man," Mankowitz says, and they stumble down the hall to the exam rooms.

A slow night. Two sisters who pulled out a hank of each other's hair over a Don Johnson poster. An assortment of lonely, aggrieved customers with articles from *Prevention* magazine and nothing to do for the evening. A woman named

Carlotta claims her eyes have changed color overnight. I tell her I believe it, though Dr. Shepard isn't nearly as interested.

Near off-shift, five to seven, is the hard part. Nina goes home at six. Gary gives in for a while. He stretches along two desks with a lab coat for a pillow, while across the room the test-pattern Indian takes up the vigil, and watches him for a change.

When the sun starts to rise, Gary and I go outside for a cigarette. I smoke only at this time of day, and only Gary's cigarettes, Lucky Strike regulars that propel me through the final hour before sleep.

Around the side of the building, we watch the sun come up over Brookline. We look out across the highway interchange and the residential district below. The air is clear and bone-chilling. I feel it carrying the smoke into my lungs.

"I still don't get it," Gary says.

"What?"

"How did Mannix get out of that warehouse? I mean, the whole place was rigged with explosives and trip wires, right?"

"Yeah."

"So, how'd he turn up in the parking lot all of a sudden?"

I have no answer for him. It's the magic of television. Beyond the highway, fog lifts off the reservoir, and the lights of the city-bound traffic grow dim as the day comes on. I drop my cigarette onto the asphalt and rub my arms for heat. Then for no reason I can understand, I say, "Mind if I ask you a question, Gary?"

"Sure," he says. "But don't ask me to explain about Mannix."

"You ever care about something so much, something that was so necessary to you—emotionally, I mean—that you think you'd just disappear if you lost it?"

He nods. "You mean something that's taken over, gotten into your sleep and eating habits."

"Yeah, like that."

"Something you can't get out of your mind, no matter what. It drives you nuts, but there's nothing you can do."

"That's it," I tell him.

He flings his cigarette into the bushes. "I don't think so," he says.

He reaches for the pack in his shirt pocket. "We'd better get back inside," I say. "Cover for me," he tells me. "One more smoke."

In front of the hospital, a man is waiting. He is in shirt sleeves, but sweating hard. "Nobody's here," he says. "Are you a doctor?"

"I can get one," I say. "Come inside."

The man precedes me indoors. "We need some help," he says. "We need a doctor." I look around for Ernie, but he's not at his stool. On the waiting-room couch, opposite Nina's desk, a young black woman sits facing the wall. From the way her shoulders move, I guess she is crying. I walk around the couch to her, and the man, hands out toward me as if to show me they're empty, says, "It was an argument. I wouldn't hurt her. It was just an argument."

There is so much blood on the woman's dress that I think she's been stabbed. She sits very quiet, staring straight ahead, and when I step in front of her I see a pulse in her forehead, and there, where her eye should be, blood pours, throbbing from a trickle to a stream down her chest and into her lap. She has a handkerchief which is soaked through completely and she holds this out to me, as if in apology for the mess she's making. "It went off in my hand," the man says, behind me now. "I just wanted to shut her up. I wouldn't hurt her."

I am calm. I tell the woman to lie down and I measure her pulse. I take off my lab coat and hold it to her head. I ask the man, calmly, when this happened and he tells me ten minutes ago. I ask the woman if she can tell me her name, does she know where she is. She tells me Vera, that she's at the hospital. I tell her to hold on, a doctor will be right here. "You're going to be all right, Vera," I tell her, and then her eye, which has been following me, goes vacant and rolls back into her head. "Don't," I say. I grab her shoulders. "Please. Don't." I run to the fire alarm behind Nina's desk and the building explodes with sound.

I have the next two days off—my weekends can crop up anywhere. Tuesday night I can't stay away. The sofa has been scrubbed and shifted forward, and two boys reach around their father's back to slap each other. Ernie, on his stool by the door, looks chastened and upright and he gives me a tight little nod, as if we've been comrades through an ordeal. Dr. Shepard tells me the man is in custody, that the woman suffered little pain before she died. I am to be nominated for a citation, he tells me. Meritorious service. I ask Nina if she has a minute, and she says she'll take a break. I have a cigarette with Ernie and then wander back to Radiology.

Nina comes in and kisses me. "I'm sorry," she says. "It must have been terrible."

"I thought she was okay," I tell her. "She was responsive. She was listening to what I said and she was watching me. I got a good pulse, a good, strong pulse. Then her eye rolled back and she wasn't there anymore."

"I'm sorry," Nina says.

"I told her to hold on. She couldn't do it."

"I guess she couldn't."

"Her name was Vera," I say.

"How do you know that?"

"She told me. She said, 'My name is Vera and I'm at the hospital. Thank you for helping me.' "

We lay out the mats and undress. Nina tells me it's okay to cry if I need to. The last time I cried is when we nearly choked Sidney Castle to death in 1967, but I don't go into that now. She is poised above me, about to guide me into her when I stop her. "I have to tell you something," I say. "I'm going to tell Lou."

She pauses; with her free hand, pulls hair from her face. "What did you say?"

"I called him. At the shop. We're having lunch on Friday."

"Lunch. You and Lou. And what are you going to tell him?"

"That I love you, Nina."

"That's good. You love me. And what do you expect Lou to say?"

"I don't know."

I am still in her hand. She tightens her grip. "You've met Lou," she says. "What do you think he's going to say?"

"I don't know, Nina. You're always saying do something. Here it is."

She slaps me away with her hand. "I wouldn't," she says. She rises, starts gathering her clothes.

"But you say you've known him forever, Nina. You say he was just always around. What about me? You know how I feel."

She stands above me. "I don't care what I've said, Cliffie. We're talking real life now, not playing in the dark."

"Is that what this is? Why do you come here then?"

"I don't know. I'm fond of you. I'm arrogant. I take whatever I can get." She kneels with her clothing in her lap

101

and takes my hand. "You're a sweet, lovely, fucked-up boy," she tells me. "I care about you very much. Don't do this."

"What else can I do, Nina? I don't know what else to do."

She pulls on her pants and leaves. The door swings wide on the lit corridor, then eases soundlessly shut. I listen until I can no longer hear her bare feet running along the tile floor.

On Wednesday, we're booked for two shows at the Dresden. Mitch is so annoyed he nearly doesn't come. Chloe is gone, along with half his record collection, forty dollars he had in a sock, and his Frisbee autographed by the Sex Pistols. She left the hole in the living-room wall. During the first show, a girl wearing a man's suit stands in front of the stage staring at him. One side of her head is shaved clean, so that it catches stage lights, while off the other, brown hair falls down her back. She dances, eyes closed, moving to a rhythm she brought in with her, because it has nothing to do with what we're playing. At intermission, Mitch buys her a beer, and when we get back on for the second set, they're gone, both Mitch and this girl. We do two songs without a drummer, and then Charlie, who plays guitar, sits in, but it's no good. We play the shortest set in history, and Charlie, in compensation, lights a towel on fire and throws it into the crowd. This is good entertainment for a few minutes, and kids toss the towel around until it's only ashes, but they know a fraud when they see one and we leave the stage to resounding boos and a shower of beer. Next morning, Charlie calls to say he hasn't heard a thing from Mitch. Neither have I, I tell Charlie.

I call Nina but she hangs up. I take the T to her house and stand across the street for two hours until three little girls come up and ask me if I'm *Spenser: For Hire*. I call Bob. He says there's a difference between positive motivational energy and Thanatos. At least it's not inertia, Bob says. We may be entering an entirely new phase in my therapy.

I find the boy at the bus stop. We have a cup of herb tea and he tells me about salvation. He has eyes like Nina's, but still, like blue glass marbles. He tells me when he found Jesus a light went on in his soul and it hasn't gone off yet. He tells me the first thought he has every morning is "Jesus loves me." From a pay phone, I call Bob in a panic, but his secretary tells me he sees his analyst Thursday afternoons.

In the paper, which I read from front to back, it said the San Andreas fault is widening, the ozone layer shrinking, and that employees of the state will soon begin using an entirely new form of English geared to improve their marketing and communication skills. The prominent vermin expert, on a fact-finding expedition to the wharves, got forty-seven bites and is at Mass General, not taking calls. The Red Sox are twenty-eight games out of first place. And the USFL, in which my mother invested heavily, has disappeared.

Friday, I come around the corner from the T, and see Lou through the restaurant window. Not until I'm inside do I see Nina, sitting opposite him in the booth. She gets up to sit next to Lou. Lou rises as well, and leans across the table to shake hands. He signals the waitress for another coffee.

I've met Lou several times, at St. Ursula's when he's come for Nina, at the Dresden, at various lectures or galleries Nina has dragged him to, where he walks or sits beside her wearing an expression of shy interest and embarrassment. He is a huge man, ten years Nina's senior, and as he grips my hand over the Formica tabletop, I can tell he is upset. Nina looks at her fingers, at her coffee, then at me, all with equal enthusiasm.

I've played this through dozens of times in my mind: Lou understands, he's known all along. He gives Nina and me his blessings and tickets to a Caribbean cruise; Lou weeps—a disturbing thing to see in a man his size—but says he would never stand in the way of Nina's happiness. No tickets in this one, but he gives us his blessing; Lou breaks down entirely, tells us he's been hitting the bottle like nobody's business. If Nina leaves, he doesn't know what he might do. I withdraw, for reasons I don't fully understand, while over a shuddering Lou, Nina looks at me with eyes full of admiration and longing.

I don't believe any of these for a minute.

I take a sip of coffee and decide not to have any more. A stimulant is not what I need. I wait for words to form. Lou leans toward me and says, "I can't do it, Cliff. I've thought it over and over, and I just don't see how I could manage."

"He really can't," Nina says, all attention now.

"You can't?" I say.

"I'd love to," Lou says, "I really would. It's been a bad year, is all. Ask me again in six months. It might be better then."

"You think so?" I say.

"Sure." Lou pats my hand with his. "Sure. You never can tell in electronics."

"You can't?" I say again, an outcome I hadn't rehearsed forming ominously in my head.

"Clifford," Nina says, "when I told Lou you were going to ask for a job at the shop, he was touched. He really was. I told him of our discussions about your future. And that a man of your potential should want to be his apprentice—I'm using his words—moved him deeply." She shrugs at me. "I guess it's been a rough year all around."

"Yes," Lou says. "It has." I nod once, twice, pour pepper into my coffee. I don't know what to do then, so I stir it in and take a sip. When I look up, Lou is reaching out to take my hand again. With his other hand, he's holding Nina's, and he brings all three of our hands together in a heap on the table. I don't look too closely, but I think his eyes are brimming with water.

"Cliff," he says, "Nina's right. I was deeply moved. And you know there's nothing in the world I wouldn't do for her. You're her friend. There's nothing in the world I wouldn't do for you."

I look at him now. Behind his glasses, little wells of water shimmer above his eyelids. Nina has brought her other hand to lie on top of the pile, and she also is getting puffy and agitated around the eyes.

"You know that, don't you?" Lou says.

"Yes," I say, adding my free hand to the stack, feeling a strange pressure myself in the eyes and throat. "I do," I tell him. I don't want to let go.

We sit like that for a moment, until we realize there's absolutely nothing we can do as long as our hands are tangled in the center of the table. We sit back, while behind the counter, the cook regards us with ill-concealed revulsion.

"You like pot roast?" Lou says. "They're famous for it here."

I hesitate. At Stevens Academy pot roast was Sunday dinner's punishment for the transgressions of the weekend.

Lou shrugs. "Why not give it a try," he says.

"All right," I say. "Sure."

Lou signals the waitress. "Three blue plates, Marge. We got a hungry group over here."

Nina digs in her purse and hands tissues all around. She smiles at me, then at Lou. "We do have another idea, Cliff," she says. "It was Lou's idea, actually, but we both thought you might hear us out."

I look over at the counter. The waitress, a woman in her forties in a yellow uniform, sits on a stool and tallies our bill. Behind the counter, the cook ladles vegetables and mashed potatoes onto three plates. He says something to the waitress and she smiles into her pad. A customer comes in and sits by them. The cook says something to him and they smile in our direction. I look at Nina and Lou, who are waiting. Then I smile too and lean back in my seat. "I'm all ears," I tell them.

From my meal with Nina and Lou, I take the T to the Public Library. By the sunny windows, under the severe gaze of a long-dead patrician, I gather my books and read until closing time: Among early plumbers were the Romans, who used lead—*plumbus*—for their piping, and gave us the word. Latrine-like receptacles with crude drains have been found in neolithic stone huts at least eight thousand years old. Some terra-cotta piping on the island of Minos is estimated to be nearly four thousand years old, and is still in good working order.

Some of the terms I come across are flange, spigot, slip joint, and screw thread. Materials vary widely, and include copper, brass, bronze, plastic, galvanized iron, wrought iron, malleable iron, and cast iron, all durable for generations of use.

On page one of *Basics in Plumbing: A Guide*, it says, "The purpose of plumbing systems is to bring into a building a supply of safe water and to collect and dispose of polluted and contaminated wastewater without hazard to the health of the occupants. Harmful chemicals and disease-producing organisms are managed and eliminated through proper drainage and venting control." I copy this part out and put it in my wallet for easy reference.

I call Tom McGinnis, head of McGinnis Brothers Plumbing and Supply. He says he can tell in two months if I've got the stuff. He says he'll sign me up for six months, after which I should know for myself. "Sign me up," I tell him.

As Steve McQueen told his sidekick, Jason, after they'd rid the town of Lucifer's Elbow of a corrupt preacher, "It ain't everything, but it's a start."

Chloe and Mitch are reconciled in San Antonio, so the band is off for now. I send a get-well card to the vermin expert and tell the boy at the bus stop his room number at Mass General. I give Bob the news and he tells me he's encouraged, and we'll talk about it next session. I leave a message on his machine saying I'll call in six months. Maybe.

Tuesday night at St. Ursula's is unusually slow, even for St. Ursula's. A new flu has hit town, and early, the waiting room fills with tribes of snifflers and sneezers, all in for throat cultures and nasal spray. Later, one woman wants to sue a granola company for putting granite in their product. ("Gran-o-la," she tells me. "Look at the *name*.") And a couple come in with documentary evidence that the Japanese are transmitting this new flu by satellite. They want a hermetically sealed room, microbe-resistant, with a view if possible.

After ten, business fades completely. The phone doesn't ring for an hour, and then it's Ernie's wife, asking if there's been any trouble. I tell her no, no trouble, and she asks me to tell Ernie to keep a sharp lookout.

When I tell Gary and Dr. Shepard I'm leaving to work for

McGinnis Brothers, they appear truly saddened. Dr. Shepard gives me his stethoscope as a gift and tells me to keep thinking about medical school, and Gary turns from the TV for ten solid minutes, missing a healthy chunk of *The Honeymooners*. He says working with me has been an exceptional joy. I tell him likewise.

At two in the morning, Mr. Friedman and Mankowitz come in, and Ernie brings Mr. Friedman to room three. He is still in the khakis and straw hat, but has put on a sweater against the October chill. The pains he had the other day were real, and not to be blamed on Mankowitz. Dr. Shepard found a mass in his belly, and he is scheduled for exploratory surgery next week. Phoenix and golf will have to wait. I take his hand and lead him to the exam table.

"What he did to me now," Mr. Friedman says.

"What? Mankowitz bothering you again?"

"The man is a devil. There is no word for mercy in his language."

"What's he done tonight?" I ask.

"Gave me soup, the bastard. Bunged me up tight as an onion. I couldn't pee if you was Cyd Charisse begging me on your knees."

Gary goes in and gives Mr. Friedman a pitcher of water to drink. I lead him to the bathroom and tell him to take his time. "Ten days, I ask the so-and-so," Mr. Friedman says, "one week. A lot to ask?" He shakes his head. I give him the sample cup and switch on the light.

Two hours later, Nina and I are in Radiology. I took my clothes off with no complaint, but declined when Nina passed me the joint. She doesn't have to tell me this is our last time. We lie on the lead mats talking, unwilling to let it end.

"Are you set with McGinnis?" she asks me.

"He said he'd try me for six months. Who knows? Maybe I'll be good at it."

"Maybe you will," Nina says.

She finishes her joint and we make love again, slowly, from various angles and vantage points. I watch her with her eyes closed and will myself to remember everything. Afterwards, she sleeps. I lie awake, thinking I should tell her it's time to dress but deciding to give her a few more minutes. The door shudders at first, then opens, splintering the darkness with hallway light. Mr. Friedman comes in, holding a small plastic cup filled with urine before him. The door closes and I hear his shallow breathing in the dark. He stands a moment, takes a deep breath, and says, "Mankowitz. You in here? I'm sorry, Mankowitz. I know it wasn't you."

I put on my pants and lead him back to the waiting room, where Mankowitz is asleep in a chair. Mr. Friedman sits in a chair next to him and picks up a magazine.

"I'll let him sleep awhile," he tells me, "then I'll take him home." Mankowitz shivers and then folds farther over his belly in sleep. "These old bastards," Mr. Friedman says, wetting a thumb to turn the pages. "They need all the help they can get."

WHAT EVERYONE WANTS

The morning rush out of Baltimore catches me by surprise, and I drive into the right lane where I can do forty-five and not be in anyone's way. I should stop, pull off the road entirely, think, but I'm too tired to do even that. At the Halethorpe entrance, a truck came within inches of me, first from behind and then to the side, blasting me with its air horn. I spilled coffee on my dress. I've got Kleenex stuffed between my legs and a cooling puddle in my left shoe. If I were a child in my parents' car, my father would pull onto the shoulder and change my clothes in full view of traffic, wiping me down with towels while my mother would busy herself with maps and lipstick, trying not to look.

I did not know what to tell Freddy. And it seems appropriate somehow, after four years of coaxing, of Freddy's assurances that we could talk anything out, that, at the last moment, I simply did not know what to say.

The call threw me; Freddy understood that. My mother has instilled in me a terror of calls that come after 11 P.M. She was a young girl alone in her parents' house when the phone rang twelve, seventeen, and, finally, thirty-four times. It was an uncle. Grandfather was dead. I would come to the door of my room when I was small, and if my father were not at home, count the rings with my mother while she put off answering.

We had spent the evening at a party in Cambridge where a Cuban poet tried to teach us all to rhumba. She had us in two lines and she called instructions over the music. There were too many people for me, and too much heat, but Freddy did remarkably well. He and the poet closed out the party with a duet that had everyone clapping.

We were home, late, and Freddy was showing me what he had learned. The phone rang while he was getting more wine. I picked it up before I could start counting the rings. It was my father.

"Sorry to call so late," he said. "I did try earlier but there was no answer."

"We just got in."

"You must be tired. I can call back."

"It's okay. Everything all right?" Freddy brought me a glass of wine and bit my bare shoulder. He lowered his head and pulled at my dress with his teeth. I pushed his face away and he rhumbaed solo into the center of the room.

"Oh, surely. Everything is all right, now. This could have waited till morning, but I thought . . ."

"Dad, what is it?"

My father does not enjoy interruptions. They confuse him. I have seen him in a college classroom when confronted with overeagerness or a flouting of decorum. He looks down and waits, just the slightest color coming into his cheeks, his hand pausing on the lectern. His silence is eloquent. You have broken the rules, it says. Now we will have to be uncomfort-

114

able until we can mend them. I watched Freddy execute a swiveling maneuver out of his pants.

"It's Mother. Her difficulties seem to have returned. She's resting now, and I'm certain the worst is behind us."

"Is she all right?"

"Oh, yes. Resting comfortably. Asleep. Rest is the essential thing now, as I'm sure you realize. Rest and time."

"Is she home?"

"No. At hospital."

My father spent a summer at Oxford before he enlisted in the Navy. He calls apartments "flats" and baby carriages "prams." He says "at hospital" and "let's have done, now." I have always felt strange when he talked that way, as if he were about to lapse into a language I wouldn't understand, and I felt it then, half out of my dress, with Freddy weaving drunkenly in front of me, uncertain what to do, with my mother deeply, calmly asleep in a darkened room somewhere, perhaps wondering if she'd done it this time, perhaps believing she had. I felt something break off inside me, allowing me to drift.

"I'll be down in the morning, Dad."

"Yes. If you could arrange it."

"Tell her. Tell her Evie will be down in the morning."

"I shall. I'll be waiting for you."

Freddy was helpful, kind. He picked up his clothing and put the wineglasses away. He put on a bathrobe and sat with me, and when it became clear I would not sleep, made a pot of coffee for both of us. When I came out of the bedroom with two suitcases packed, he looked at me but didn't show any surprise. It was then I realized I didn't know what to say. I let him hold me and then I held him, too, and then he carried the suitcases to my car. He said, "Drive carefully. You're tired."

If he'd said another word to me, anything, maybe I would have asked him to come.

The man in the tollbooth notices my skirt hiked up to my thighs. He leans far out of the window to hand me my change. I drive through my parents' neighborhood and feel that if I closed my eyes, my car, horse-like, would know the way home. I make the quick illegal turn off the exit ramp, and pass the younger sister of a high school classmate, grown now, dressed like a secretary, blinking her eyes sleepily at the bus stop. In front of the bakery, Mrs. Teaman waves at me as though she still sees me every day, and at the car wash, the black boys stand with their dripping rags, checking me out as they do every female pausing for the traffic signal. I pass the wide grounds of my school where the high morning light seems especially full and serene, and I watch little girls in plaid jumpers jostle each other through a break in the playing-field hedge. I know every house, know to slow down crossing the Sage Avenue bridge, and by the time I pull onto their street and catch sight of the peonies and wisteria, the blue hydrangeas, I am tensed with a rage that frightens me. I turn into the driveway just as my father steps out the door. I shut off the ignition and listen to faint ticking as the engine contracts.

My parents fell in love the year of Pearl Harbor. My mother was an Art History student at a small women's college north of Manhattan, where, to her often professed surprise, two articles she wrote on Tintoretto were published in respected journals. On the day they were married, she was to have traveled to the Rutgers campus in Livingston, New Jersey, to present a talk on "Iconography in Mannerist Painting." She wired the organizers of the conference, demurely asking their congratulations, certain they would understand. The organizers never replied.

Marriage spread like a spring virus through the Marycrest campus in 1941. Things much more serious than college seemed to be in the air, and the girls felt they had to grow up overnight. The parties were gayer, my mother has told me, they lasted sometimes until dawn, and the young men in their uniforms stood in groups under the trees, and were unendurably beautiful.

My father was older than most of the men; already twenty-nine, he was finishing his Ph.D. in Political Science at Yale and awaiting his commission in the Navy. He did not smoke cigarettes like the rest of the young men, who sucked on them with heavy lips, and jabbed them in the air until you could feel smoke on your skin and hair. He drank, but quietly. When the boys sang fight songs, he didn't join in, and he spoke of the likelihood of going to war with a calm seriousness that made my mother feel strong. He was quite handsome when she made him take off his glasses, and he could dance like no one she had ever met. His touch was wonderfully light, his anticipation, flawless. I could believe it or not, my mother has said, but from the first time he held her on the dance floor, when he leaned toward her as they waited for the music, she knew they would marry. And she was certain he did, too.

The ceremony took place in the Marycrest chapel. My father had just received his ensign's bars, and in the wedding pictures he looks as crisp and bright as his new uniform. He is much taller than my mother, a large man, and in the pictures he is leaning solicitously over her shoulder, leading her gently by the arm. She is beautiful: small and trim and camera-shy.

In the posed shots by the cake and the chapel door, he is laughing at the camera, and she is looking up at him.

Great-aunt May's money paid for the wedding, as it had mother's tuition fees. Aunt May was a woman of remarkable energy who dressed in rough tweed suits and hats, and taunted her husband that she would be spending his railroad money fifty years after he was in the ground. She was right only by half. When it was time for my mother to go to college, she wrote my grandparents, insisting on Marycrest, announcing that illiterate girls attracted second-rate husbands.

At the reception, she had a chair carried out to one of the chestnut trees on the lawn, where she sat smoking, and where she was joined for a time by Professor Carlisle of the Art History Department. The poor man was inconsolable, she told my mother. The entire discipline, apparently, had expected greatness from Margaret Connors.

"An absolutely bizarre little man," Aunt May said. "Can you really assume, I asked, that a girl of Margaret's age and personal attractiveness, who has seen a bit of life, though I grant you, just a bit—am I to understand that you expect her to throw aside all the possibilities and join you in your cellars or libraries, or wherever it is you congregate, to take measurements and develop squints, while the world just passes her by? Do you, I inquired, really? You can imagine, my dear, he had nothing to say."

I am in the breakfast room, drinking coffee. It is early still to go to the hospital. My father has filled the electric percolator, making enough coffee for twelve people, and is blundering around the kitchen like a bear in a campsite. I am too tired, if he expects me to go in and take over, and he can see me to a cup of coffee after I've driven all night.

The breakfast room is all windows and lemon wallpaper. Like all the rooms, it was arranged by my mother and the decorator with a specific ambience in mind. This room was to be "cheery"; my mother has always felt it essential to begin the day in a cheery atmosphere. I would sit here on school-day mornings and watch her domestic fury, a whirling apron with six arms ending variously in pot holders, spatulas, egg cups, napkin rings. Flipping the eggs, or the pancakes, she would reduce the flame under the coffee to simmer, and as I watched the blue jets diminish, before I had seen her turn, pour the juice and slap jelly into a crystal dish. Flowers were already on the table, mail, if any, by the side of your plate. If an egg over-easy burst, she put it aside for herself, and if a piece of toast charred, she scraped it over the sink as if dirt had got onto the bread. Breakfast is the most important meal of the day, she would say. Watching her, I could never eat. When I told her that Fred and I, as a rule, avoided each other in the mornings and preferred a doughnut and coffee at work, she worried about our relationship for weeks.

Breakfast is the most important meal of the day, she would say. Little strokes fell great oaks. Boys never make passes at girls who wear glasses.

My father comes in and sits down. I have told him I don't want anything to eat and he has made himself scrambled eggs and toast. Black flecks are mixed in with the yellow, and there is a faint smell of ash in the air. He offers me more coffee.

"Are you sure you won't have something to eat?" he says. "What will I tell your mother?"

I take more coffee. Uncharacteristically, my father has not dressed for breakfast. He is past sixty and growing jowls. On his face, and on his chest, which I see through the bathrobe as he leans over the eggs, the skin sags as if the flesh under it has come unattached and is sliding. He is growing breasts and jowls. The sharp young ensign with the magazine smile has body hair growing in thickets on his shoulders and upper arms. I feel guilty about the eggs.

"How's Fred?"

"Fine. On the ascent. There are rumblings about making him a partner."

"Well, I am not surprised. I've always believed a bright young man with an exact knowledge of what he desires is almost impossible to hold down."

"Yes."

"And your work? How has that been?"

"The same."

I am an assistant editor at a small publishing house in Boston. My job is to write jacket copy. I say things like: "The author, a well-loved gourmand in her native Sydney, travels the world in search of the perfect chocolate confection. Readers will be smacking their lips." In publishing, they tell me it's not what you do, it's how you get your foot in the door.

My father returns to his eggs. And what about a bright young woman with only an exact knowledge of what she doesn't want, I say, but to myself. To him I say, "I'm thinking of quitting. Leaving Boston."

"Yes? And Fred?"

"He's staying."

He reaches for the jam. "Plans?"

"I thought I might go stay with a friend in Durham for a few days. She lives outside of town, in the country. She's invited me."

"And your job?"

"Freddy's going to give them a call."

"I see."

I have been talking to the top of my father's head as he

labors over his toast, covering the bread with loving strokes of the knife.

"Then I thought I'd coach women's field hockey for a while, or make fabric softener commercials. Something feminine but dignified, you know? Make some money and retire in time to have a great man's child."

He looks up now, blankly, and without animation, his face settles into creases and a half day's beard. I realize suddenly he has not slept either. He puts the uneaten toast on his plate. I have not apologized to my father in years, and am unable to now. I try, instead, to soften my voice.

"How's Mother?"

"As I told you. Resting comfortably. Cheerful, when I spoke to her last. She seems to react to these experiences as though they were vacations."

"Did she ask for her housecoat?"

"Yes. And slippers and makeup kit. I took them all down last night so she would have them when she awoke."

"How's her throat, and her stomach?"

He sweeps crumbs toward his plate with a napkin. "They didn't pump her stomach this time," he says.

"Why? Didn't she take enough? I thought they did it as a precaution."

"She didn't take pills, Eve."

My mother has been hospitalized twice before for suicide attempts. Both times, she took enough pills to make her very sick, not enough to kill. I always pictured her cold-creaming her face, washing her hands, brushing her hair, and getting into bed before swallowing the pills with water from the bedside tumbler. If she did die, if she intended to at all, she would be found among order, clean and fresh in her own bed, a decorous woman.

"What do you mean?" I say.

"She didn't take pills. She took a scissors, in the bathtub. She tried to cut her throat."

He looks for me to respond. The coffee is making me sick, the coffee and sunlight in this yellow room.

"I found her in the tub. I believe she meant to turn on the water but forgot. I think it's supposed to ease the pain, the water. She was calling me. I don't know how long before I heard. There was blood. It was difficult to lift her."

I don't know what to do with my hands. They touch the cup, the sugar, come up to my face and down again. I close my eyes so as not to hear.

"Doctor says it's not much of a cut. Missed anything major. The drama in these cases is to be expected, he says. An appeal, like the pills, but more so. There will be a scar, I'm afraid."

My mother's bathroom is an ensemble of greens. The paper is delicate lime with a foreground of interlacing white bamboo. The shower curtain is deep pine, and the buffed emerald carpeting, a rare and expensive Danish weave. The towels are simple pastels, designed to blend, and the porcelain, palest mauve, offsets the rest. My father is looking at me, the apologetic smile, waiting. I take his cup and saucer, and mine, and go into the kitchen.

"We should go soon," I say. "I'll wash up."

It was a stupid thing. I was overheated and tired, we had been hiking for several hours, and though the rock looked unsteady, I put my foot down on it anyway. I fell, and narrowly missed hitting my head on a larger rock by the side of the trail. My ankle swelled immediately, enough that we decided to turn back without reaching the summit.

"Are you all right?" Freddy said. "Can you walk on it?"

"I'm all right."

Two miles down the trail, I sat down abruptly on a log. My vision refused to focus and objects were outlined in white. Pains shot from my ankle all the way up my side. The skin had now turned purple, and when I pulled the jeans over my calf, a gash-like bruise stretched to where a piece of flesh seemed to jut.

"Jesus," Fred said. He whistled under his breath and put a hand to his mouth. I didn't look at him anymore. Then he put his arms around me from behind and started to lift.

"Don't," I said.

"Eve, you can't walk on that." He began pulling me up. I brought both elbows back sharply into his chest.

"Don't."

He let go. "I'm just trying to help you," he said.

"Don't help me. I can walk. I don't want your help."

In the tent, I lay on a sleeping bag and cried while Freddy called a doctor. I was completely embarrassed. The doctor came in an ambulance, and all the campers from the surrounding sites gathered as I was lifted onto a gurney. I had broken my leg in two places, and from walking on it, had compressed one fracture badly.

The doctor said, "You've behaved like a fool. You may have done yourself permanent harm."

On the way to the hospital, Freddy sat with me in place of the attendant. They had given me something which was making me drowsy, but I didn't sleep. I remember he sat on the stool with his back to me, and did not look away from the window once.

My mother sings out, "Just a minute," as if we've come to the door at a dinner party. We go in and she is sitting up in bed. A wide white bandage is taped to her neck, and her hair, stiff and jutting at angles from sleep, has just been brushed.

"Evie." She holds her arms out. When I come close, she brings her hands together on mine and lets me lean over. She kisses the air to the side of my cheek. "Darling."

At a table in the corner, my father arranges the flowers we brought. He seems dissatisfied, first with the vase we picked up at the nurses' station, then with the way the flowers hang. He takes off his coat and folds it over the back of a chair.

"You look well, dear," my mother says.

"Yes, Evie and I have had a fine breakfast. It missed only you, Margaret."

"Did you give her something to eat, Arthur? There was a nice piece of ham I bought."

"I wasn't hungry, Mom."

"Eve, dear, you know how I feel about breakfast. You've got to start your day off well."

My mother is a thin woman with wonderful eyes and skin, and the mannerisms of a startled bird. When she talks, more when she listens, her eyes flit across your face to the corners of the room, and her smile, while never disappearing, never quite establishes itself. Her beauty is not strong. I have inherited my father's strength; what beauty I possess is durable. People have described my face as having character. My mother's beauty is of a different type. It should be seen in tableaux, among other beautiful things, framed at the top of the stairs with the sun over her shoulder, in a yard swing in autumn, endlessly rocking. She is chipped at, scarred. I would fold her in my arms but she is ashamed of the bandage. She is trying to make us comfortable. She smiles.

"Doctor says we are doing marvelously this morning."

"We?" my father asks.

124

"Yes. I suppose he meant me, or his other patients, too. Maybe everyone. Is it nice outdoors?"

"Yes," my father says. "It seems to be shaping up."

"Good. Maybe they'll take me for a walk later, if the sun isn't too strong. Mrs. Hull, she's the day nurse, she noticed my complexion right away. She said skin like mine needs constant care, constant attention. I like her very much."

"Did the doctor say anything else, Margaret?"

"Anything else? Yes, I'm sure he must have. We had quite a nice talk. Let me think. He said I mustn't worry about a thing. He said if any of the nurses told him I was worrying, he would come right down and be cross with me. And I said, 'But Doctor, how am I not to worry about that?' "

She laughs, and my father smiles. I am still holding her hands. She picks mine off the blanket and grips them. "Eve, darling. It's so good to see you. Tell me how you are. Tell me about Fred. Has he shaken that awful cold?"

"Yes, I think so. I think he has."

"Tell him I wasn't joking about the rosemary. He's not a full partner yet, is he? He can listen to some advice, even from a foolish old lady."

"He always listens to you, Mom. You know that."

"A marvelous boy. I'm so happy for the two of you. I've told you that, haven't I? So happy."

My mother begins to hum, smiling at us, as if we should join in. My father looks away. I say, "So how are you, Mom? I mean, how do you feel?"

She stops humming abruptly. "Feel? Oh, me," she sighs. "I feel fine, though I can't say I'm entirely pleased with the room. There's no sun at all in the morning, and then after lunch, it comes blazing through all the windows at once.

125

Blinds don't touch it. I haven't said anything, though. I wouldn't want to complain."

"Are you getting enough rest?"

"Oh, yes. Sleeping much too much, though. A great *deal* too much, I should think. And the funny thing is, with all this sleep, I'm still tired. Exhausted. I can't understand it, can you? Why, as I remember, I wasn't nearly as tired the other times." She brings a hand to her mouth. She looks quickly from me to my father, frightened. I stroke her other hand.

"We're here, Mom. I'm going to stay with Dad a few days. I've arranged it at work." She looks at me and then down at the blankets. The hand I've been holding she now raises to her neck, shielding the bandage. "I've got time, Mother. I want it for us." She doesn't look at me.

We stay until they bring her lunch. My father reads the newspaper and calls out the interesting items. He wonders how many people are aware that there are six separate wars going on in the world at this moment. My mother stares into a romance she has borrowed from Mrs. Hull. Every few moments, she closes her eyes, and when she opens them says, "I wasn't sleeping, was I?"

Before we leave, my father says, "Dear, has Evie told you about the coffee? It was a funny thing. I'm ashamed to say it, but after all these years, I still cannot operate that machine. It seems I made enough to last a week. *And* I burned the eggs." They both laugh. "Eve has extracted a solemn promise from me not to do the laundry, and by no means attempt any manipulation of the gas range. We are all in a fuddle, dear. The cats are morose, the plants miss you, and I miss you, too. We all want you home."

*   *   *

It is a standing joke of my parents that my mother makes the world's best martinis. Downstairs at six, showered and scented, she would have the drinks ready when my father walked through the door at a quarter past. They would have one each and he would compliment her. If all else failed, he would say, if the university burned and the economy collapsed, she could support them tending bar. If his mood were especially gay, he'd have her mix up a couple more and he would take her on his lap to watch the evening news. She always made the drinks, even at their parties, and when the inevitable praise came, she laughed. When I grew old enough to know a good martini from a bad, I knew my mother's were bad, and that everyone else knew it, but they still had her make the drinks.

The troubles began when I was in high school. We went through three postmen in a month after my mother accused them of peering through the windows. She took the milk box out to the edge of the lawn and had both milk and mail deposited there, so no one would come up to the house. Her sleeping patterns became erratic. Sometimes, I would come home from school to find her still in bed, other times she would be up all night. She woke me one morning at 4 A.M. to ask if I remembered the recipe for the cranberry biscuits we had on Thanksgiving. She cleaned the basement, throwing out, among other things, all her college papers, photographs, and books. She smelled mold growing in them, she said.

On a Sunday, we were sitting down to dinner. My parents had had drinks in the living room and I had been given a poem by Tennyson to read aloud before the start of the meal. The candles had been lit, and the fire; the curtains were drawn against the dark street. My father and I were at the table. The warmth, and the reflections of the wine, crystal, and candlelight in the polished wood, gave me a familiar floating sensation. My father carved the roast and laid the slices carefully on a serving dish, never looking up, never pausing until the task was completed.

At first, the sound was soft, as if, in the kitchen, my mother were laughing to herself, or just catching her breath. Then it grew louder and didn't stop, and I was frightened because I had never heard a person make a sound like that. My father stood at the meat platter, knife and fork over the roast, listening. I waited for him to go in and help her stop crying. He brought his hands slowly down to his sides and did not move. I waited for him to go to her.

In the afternoon, my father goes to his office at the university. I go home and take two steaks out of the freezer. I have told him I will make us a fine meal, and he is to stop at Lerner's on the way back and buy the best Beaujolais in the store.

The house feels big when I am in it alone. It's been too long since it was my home for me to reclaim it without someone there to invite me. They've put a bookcase in my room, filled with *National Geographics* and *Reader's Digest* condensed novels, and my mother's sewing machine is now by the window, where my desk used to be. My photographs are still hanging, and in the drawers are my letters and diaries, but I look at them with faint recognition, as if they are someone else's things that I have seen before.

It is only two in the afternoon, but I pour myself a large bourbon from the mahogany cabinet in the den. I don't usually drink bourbon; my father says women don't like the taste. I find an old Stones album and put it on the stereo. It echoes loudly in this room where Bach and Gabrielli are usually played. I sit on the sofa with the two cats in my lap, put my head back, and sing.

Later, I have another drink, and water the plants. I vacuum the downstairs, though I can see not a speck of dirt anywhere, and I dust the bookshelves and tabletops. At three, I call Freddy in his office.

"It's me, Fred."

"Eve. How are you? How's your mom?"

"Fine. Radiant. She does these things so well."

"Did the procedure upset her?" He is talking about the stomach pump. I decide not to tell him the truth.

"No, not too bad. Not too bad. Alfred, sweet, is Monica in the room?" Monica is his secretary.

"It's Frederick, darling, always has been. As a matter of fact, yes. Why?"

"It's just, Al, I was wondering if you wanted to fuck me."

"Eve, dear, how nice. But you know how difficult these things are over the phone."

"I've got my shirt off."

"Do you? Let me look into that."

"I just put my tongue in your ear. Feel it?"

"Is that it? Yes, I think I do. Thanks so much."

"Are you getting hard?"

"Yes, dear. These things are extremely hard. I miss you."

"It's lonely down here, Alfred."

"Here, too."

"I told Mother I'd stay. A few days."

"That sounds like a good idea. I called your office. They understand."

"Freddy. I'm sorry about . . ." I can't think of the end to the sentence. "I'm sorry."

129

He waits, then puts his hand over the receiver and I hear muffled talk. He takes his hand away.

"How are you, Eve?" he says.

"I don't know. Okay."

"How's your father taking it?"

"All right. It's strange without my mother. We haven't really talked."

"I sent your mother flowers. I didn't know if I should, but I thought she might like them."

The phone call isn't working. I feel lonelier than before and I haven't made Freddy any happier. I don't say anything. A buzzer goes off in his office and he has to put me on hold. After a moment, I hear the line reconnect, though he doesn't speak.

"Eve," he says, finally. "Whatever you decide. Take as long as you need. If you want, I'll be here."

I finish the second drink and go up to my parents' room. My father's side of the bed is unevenly made, my mother's, smooth and untouched. On the dressing table, my mother has an assortment of tubes and bottles that would last me several lifetimes. I dab some perfume on my neck; it is cold. I open my mother's closet. She has forty-one pairs of shoes. I count them. I walk into the closet and push between the dresses. The scent of her, fine at first, makes me dizzy.

I lie on her part of the bed and pull the satin comforter over me. I roll onto my side, undo my jeans, and put my hand between my legs. I think that it's three in the afternoon on a Thursday and I'm drunk. I think of Freddy, and my parents dancing on a polished hardwood floor. When I finish, I close my eyes and sleep.

After my mother's first illness, Aunt May came to stay with us. She arrived on a Sunday afternoon in her blue

Packard, and stood on the sidewalk as if it were the deck of a steamship while her chauffeur carried the bags indoors. Without checking to see what we had, she sent Hillary, the chauffeur, to the market for a refrigerator-load of food, and when he returned, to the florist for a roomful of bouquets. When my mother came home from the hospital the following day, she brought the flowers she had been given by the Faculty Wives and the Neighborhood Merchant's Association. But these were small, and starting to turn, and after seating my mother on the back porch for the breeze, Aunt May had me take them out to the trash.

Aunt May took the situation in hand. In her day, she told us, families pulled together in times of emotional or natural disaster. From her chair in the living room, she directed my mother's convalescence like a general orchestrating a campaign.

For my mother, she prescribed naps after lunch and before dinner, and tepid baths twice a day for twenty minutes, precisely. She treated the water with a special powder given her by a homeopath in Tangier. She had personally seen it cure a young girl of polio or some Arab thing.

Reading was considered therapeutic, and Hillary was kept in a constant shuttle to the public library, and Aunt May, occupied in choosing appropriate titles. She described her requirements: "Nothing torrid or adventurous; nothing with ridiculous people in sticky relations; nothing that involves politics or children or foreign travel."

I was kept close. I was to change my mother's drinking water and make certain she did not close the windows. I was to coax her into the sunlight and watch she didn't burn, lure her into the night air and see she didn't chill, ask her to go walking and make sure she didn't tire. Otherwise, I could sit by Aunt May and hold her reading glasses or teacup, as if a fourteen-year-old girl's single desire was to touch a rich lady's belongings.

My father was quiet, apparently happy to give Aunt May charge of the house. She showed a particular patience toward him, called him "your poor father," and at night, after Mother and I had been sent to bed, sat up with him to discuss my mother's progress. She would arrange that my parents had time together, leaving them on the front porch after dinner, taking me inside to read to her. Through the living-room window, I would see them on the wicker couch, looking into the night, demure and hesitant as a newly introduced couple. My father slept in the den so my mother could rest undisturbed, and Aunt May had me serve him a pot of black coffee there in the mornings, because men like to start their days alone.

One weekend, Aunt May announced that if the weather was reasonable, we would take a trip to the beach. The weather was, and with my parents and Aunt May in the rear, and me with silent Hillary and the food basket up front, we set out in the Packard to Horseneck Beach.

Though late in the spring, it was a chilly day, with a wind coming off the water. The beach was deserted except for a couple down by the sand flats. The man called out something and waved at us with a bottle of wine, but we turned our backs and walked toward the cove.

Hillary handed out blankets and sweaters, and set up two wooden chairs. He returned to the car for the food and books. Aunt May began telling my mother about a colonel she knew on Nantucket who cured a lifelong neuralgia by sailing on the *Queen Mary* every summer and sticking his head out of his cabin porthole into the full sea breeze for forty-five minutes a day. He had been written up in an encyclopedia. I said I would walk to the ridge at the end of the beach to see the lighthouse, and my father, perhaps because no chair had been set up for him, said he would come along.

I walked by the edge of the water, looking for shells and bits of sea glass. When I found one I thought particularly nice, I brought it to my father. He held the best ones for me in his jacket pocket, and threw the others into the waves. We reached the escarpment. I climbed to the top and waited for him to follow. We sat on the higher rocks overlooking the cove, and the lighthouse and Coast Guard station, both deserted since the Second World War. My father turned his pockets out and gave me back the shells and glass. I looked at them one by one, and threw them down the rocks at the water.

"I thought you would want those," he said. "They were pretty ones."

"Why is she here?" I said.

"Who?"

"Why did she have to come? We don't need her."

"If you mean Aunt May, Eve, she didn't have to come, but I'm not at all certain we don't need her."

"Why?"

"She's very close with your mother, dear. In some ways, she brought your mother up. It's hard to explain. Mother has been quite ill and it means a great deal to her to have Aunt May here with us."

"She took pills."

"What?" He turned to me, smiling, quietly stunned, as if I were an infant and had just spoken my first word.

"I know she took pills. I found them. They were all over the blankets after you left for the hospital."

"Evie." He was still smiling. "That was medicine. That was mother's medicine."

I took the remaining shells in my hand and threw them hard on the rocks.

"She tried to kill herself. I knew it that night. She needs us and you've brought Aunt May here to make believe it's all something else."

He tried to reach out to me but I stood up and turned away. I spoke into the wind, with my back toward my father, and I was no longer certain I even wanted him to hear. "What did we do to her? How could she be so sad?"

He was close enough now to hear; I could feel him right behind me.

"We haven't done anything. We love your mother. Don't you think she knows that?"

Back on the beach side, the weather was turning. Over the water, gray clouds were changing shape and the wind, stronger, blew scudding shreds of foam onto the sand. I walked quickly, gathered my hair into the collar of my sweatshirt, and did not look up when my father came up beside me. Ahead, we could see Aunt May wrapped like a package in her chair, brief ribbons of smoke whipping away from her cigarette. The couple was gone. My mother had left her seat and was standing by the water's edge. As we came closer, I saw her hands white against the shoulders of her sweater, and her knees moving.

"What happened?" my father said. "What's wrong?"

Aunt May looked up from her reading. "Wrong? What do you mean? You know exactly what's wrong. We were talking. Or I, at least, was making an attempt. She started to cry. I asked what the trouble was and she wouldn't answer. I gave her a handkerchief. I said, cry, if you think that will do any good. Cry through lunch. Cry until breakfast. We all have time. Cry."

"But what is it? What got her upset?"

"How am I to know, Arthur? We will allow her her little hysteria, and then, if she would like, the three of us will sit calmly and discuss it."

My mother stood ten or fifteen yards from us. I was not certain if she could hear them talking. My father sat heavily in the empty chair and stared out at the sea. A wave came in fast, its white lip curling up the sand. My mother didn't move and the water foamed over her shoes, leaving them partially buried as it receded. She had her hands wrapped around her shoulders like someone freezing to death. She turned her back to us and began walking. I caught up to her and reached for one of her hands, reddening with cold. She didn't respond. I put my hands in my sweatshirt and fell in step with her, our feet pressing pale crescents out in the wet sand before us. White tips were lifting off the water and the horizon was a deeply lit slate. It would rain, but maybe not right away. The beach was long in this direction; I had never found its limit. If the rain held up, I thought, we could walk away from them for hours.

Everything is ready. I have turned the steaks, changed the flowers, culled the brightest peppers and tomatoes from my mother's garden for a salad. My father comes in quietly, as if entering a room where someone is sleeping. He stops to look at me, hands me the Beaujolais, and goes upstairs.

I stand in the middle of the room with the bottle in my hand. I am wearing a summer dress of my mother's, and a pair of her shoes. We are the same size, and she is always pressing me to take some of her clothes to Boston. I have washed my hair and pulled it back with combs, and I have even found a perfume among hers that I thought suited me. I thought I looked very nice and he has made me feel naked. He will not do this to me, I say. He will not leave me here, with the table set and the food ready. He will not do this. I say this to myself, preparing it for him. I am about to follow him up the stairs when he comes out of his room in a dinner jacket and fresh shirt, hair cleanly brushed, smiling like a young lover.

We are shy with each other at the table. He pulls my chair out, and passes me the cork from the bottle to sniff. We murmur appreciation for the wine, hold our glasses up to the light, and when we eat, my father is careful to comment about the steak, the salad, the potatoes, the bread. My mother is usually here to supply the conversation, to bridge the distance between husband and child. She knows the names of his colleagues at the university, the agenda of his upcoming faculty meeting, and what Freddy likes to call me when he's drunk. She knows precisely how long to laugh at jokes, to be instantly attentive when necessary, to draw all ends of the conversation into the center. Without her, we are formal; it is her house, finally, and my father and I are guests whose host has disappeared.

When the wine is finished, my father goes to the cabinet for another bottle. I am surprised, having prepared myself to say I'd had plenty with one. The bottle is from Aunt May's stock, one of the few remaining. I recognize the label, though he tries to hide it from me.

"Eve," my father says. "This is wonderful."

"You always knew your steak, Dad."

"Yes, but I had no idea you could cook this way. I envy Fred his meals."

"You should," I say. "He cooks most of them."

The cork is hard to remove and my father does something I have never seen before. He takes the bottle and clamps it between his knees. His face contorts with the exertion, and when the cork comes away with a loud pop, we both laugh. His expression then is also new to me: jovial, slack, nearly intimate.

"Your great-aunt carries her influence even into the grave," he says. "I always suspected she would have liked to take the wine with her."

We drink, and I am again surprised when my father keeps my glass full. Slowly, in the heady glow of Aunt May's vintage stock, I feel myself relax, feel the quiet buoyancy of Sunday-night dinners when I was a child. My father asks if I would like some music. He goes to the phonograph, where the Stones album I played is still on the turntable.

"I thought I fed all of these to the cats," he says, and puts on a Beethoven sonata. He returns to the table.

"You know, for years I thought your mother was quite an imbecile. She always preferred these early works to the "Hammerklavier" or the Sonata in A. She preferred early Schubert, too, and I was always very disturbed and embarrassed. Imagine my shock, then, when a few years back, I found I preferred them myself. I remember, when I finally braced myself to tell her, she said nothing, but smiled and seemed to gain several inches in height before my eyes. Didn't say a word, your mother, just grew taller."

We listen to the music in silence. When the sonata is done, my father pours wine into our glasses. He stands. "What would you say to this, Eve?" he says, and puts an album on the stereo. A waltz. My father straightens his back and extends a hand toward me.

We dance between the stereo and the couch, between the dining room and the bookcases. There is not much room to dance really, but I relax into my father's lead, filled with the wine and the music, and we don't come near to hitting anything, we don't have a problem with the furniture at all. We dance. Thoughts go through my brain randomly, at angles, like the reflections of light as we turn. I have to tell my father I am learning to rhumba. I will suggest we finish off as much of Aunt May's wine as we can and break the rest of the bottles in the fireplace. We should go to the hospital, I think, sneak into Mother's room and get her to dance. She would love to, it would be all she really needed. I will call Freddy, wake him up, tell him I don't know what all the trouble was, I don't know where it came from. I will tell my father the same, everyone, the same.

We stop, finally, breathless, and the room about us locks back into distinctness. Leaning on my father's chest, I see us in the mirrors by the staircase, my father flushed but erect, getting his wind, and me in his arms, hair coming loose from my mother's combs, her dress wrapped around my legs, her perfume lifting off my breasts to fill my brain.

"Well," my father says. "Perhaps we should sit one out."

I sit on the sofa and he brings me my wine. He sets his own glass beside mine, and goes to turn down the volume of the music. When he comes back, he is smiling.

"Would it be overdramatic for me to say how good it is to have you home?"

I smile and shake my head. He reaches for his glass and listens, his upper body still in sway to the music. He offers me the handkerchief from his pocket and I shake my head again. He mops his face and puts the cloth away. The whirling has not quite subsided in me, and I cannot free myself of our image in the mirror. I have had too much wine. Freddy would have known not to let me drink so much. I fight being drunk. My father leans toward me.

"Eve. There is something I wanted to discuss with you. This seems a good time."

The record comes to an end and we listen to the machine turn itself off as though it were part of the music. Then my father says, "It's about Fred. About what you said this morning."

He looks for me to respond. The sweat has returned already to his face and in this light, or in my vision, he looks old again. I wonder if the dancing was too much for him, if I shouldn't have stopped us sooner.

"I was very disturbed by it. You said you were leaving him. Isn't that true?"

I don't speak. I drink from my glass of wine.

"Why?" he says. "Can you tell me why?"

I empty the glass and set it on the table between us. I look at him, but he is not about to fill it this time. That portion of the evening's entertainment is over. I go into the dining room for the bottle myself. He follows me.

"I don't understand," he says. "I would like to, your mother and I would both like to understand. He seems a fine young man with a future. You seemed happy with him, I thought, until now."

I sit at the table with the steak remains and the crystal and silver reflections in the candlelight. I begin to float, to cry, to leap through the latticed windows out onto the street. I fight it.

"I was happy," I say.

He sits in his chair. "Yes?" he says. "And now?"

"Now, I'm leaving."

"What is this, Eve? A game? What are you playing at? This isn't a game anymore. I don't see what you want."

An exact knowledge. My father sits back, quietly exasperated, and lifts a hand to his tie. He pinches the knot between thumb and forefinger, and moves it away from his throat, a habit I have seen countless times. But this time a memory floods through me. I am a young girl, six or seven years old, dressed in a new Easter outfit: dirndl skirt with petticoats, blue jacket, white blouse and hat. A purse for shiny quarters. My mother is waiting in the car, and I am looking for my father at the university. The doors all look the same. I am directed to a room at the end of the hall. I push a brass bar over my head, and a group of men, my father among them, is standing beside a long table. The door closes behind me, and the men look up. I remember what my mother showed me in the store. Gathering my skirt in my hands, I pull it forward and dip at the knees, careful to hold my feet at right angles. The man nearest me puts a hand to his waist and bows deeply. I repeat my performance, and when another man bows stiffly from the shoulders, I go around the circle, one by one, holding my skirt in my fingers, putting one shiny Mary Jane behind the other the way my mother showed me. Each of the men greets me in turn; they smile at my father. It is late in the afternoon, and I've had an exciting day. My father pinches his tie. The men are all laughing, and then I am too, topping their boisterous shouts with girlish delight.

"Eve." My father puts a hand out on the tablecloth. I look at him, laughter ringing off in my head. "What is it? Can we talk about it?"

"I don't want to love him."

"What?" He looks as if he will laugh in my face. "What do you mean by that?"

"I don't want to love Freddy."

He does laugh now, almost happily. "But why? What are

you? Solitary? Made of stone? Come on, dear, I know what you want."

"What, Dad?"

"What we all want, I should think. A home, someone to share it, a few comforts, possessions, a family at some point. We all want that, don't we? That's what everyone wants."

"I don't want any of it."

"Then you're a fool. Then you don't know anything."

He gathers his plate and silverware and carries them into the kitchen. The slight breeze off his jacket as he passes feels like his hand sharp on my face. I hold on to the table edge; I fight it.

The table in front of me has lengthened, the perspective of the room altered. The plates, the glasses and flowers, have taken on the clarity and chromatic brilliance of a vision. I am not drunk, now. There is movement inside me. I am a house being shut up for the winter; someone is walking through me methodically slamming all the windows. I think: this man's wife is lying in a hospital bed with stitches in her throat.

I feel him right behind me; I wait for his touch on my back. "I apologize," he says. "Let's try again, shall we? It's something I've learned from your mother. No matter what happens, you can always try again."

All at once, I have too many words to say. They rush at my mouth from my chest, my stomach. My throat swells with them. I lean forward and bring my head to my knees, waiting for strength to leave the room.

My mother doesn't understand. Her hair is wrapped in a towel, still wet, and her fingernails, newly painted, are splayed evenly across the table in front of her. She smiles politely, patiently. Finally, my father tries to explain.

"Margaret," he says. "It's been wonderful having Evie home. But the doctors say it will be at least two weeks before any changes can be made in your treatment, and what they have in mind afterwards, we still don't know. Eve must attend to plans she has made in Durham. Frankly, I am falling terribly behind in my work. We thought it sensible for Eve to come back later, when we're all at home and you've had a good rest."

She turns her smile to me and nods. Not moving her hands, she reminds me of a puppet, a mechanical doll with its head on a swivel. I find it hard to look at her.

"Is Fred going to meet you in Durham?" she says. I shake my head. "Well, Eve. You know, by the time you come back, we'll have the new paper in the dining room, and I hope, though I really can't predict, a new floor in the kitchen. Have you called Mr. Seymour, dear?"

"I forgot, Margaret," my father says. "I will this afternoon."

"Make certain he understands I will not accept Ivory this time." She raises her eyebrows. "Why, last time, I invited Mr. Seymour to tea, I believe I made sandwiches, and for hours we sat and examined color charts, paint chips, molding designs. I had the worst trouble making up my mind. But finally, I did. Madagascar White. Well. Guess what I saw on the walls the next day, already dry over by the hutch? Can you guess? I said, 'Mr. Seymour. If I had wanted Ivory, do you think I would have spent an entire week deciding on Madagascar White?' "

The morning sun has just reached the windows. A nurse comes in and adjusts the blinds.

"I'll call every day, Mom." I take one of her hands, careful of the nail polish. "We'll discuss the paper in the dining room. I've got some opinions you might like to hear."

She nods gladly, eyes bright with drugs. I stroke her fine small hand.

"Well, Missus, shall we make you beautiful for your family today?"

The nurse has come over to the bed. She is a stocky black woman, with sleeves rolled up. She waits, bouncing slightly on her gum-soled shoes. I stand.

"Mrs. Hull, you've met my husband. This is our daughter, Eve."

She smiles. "Now," she says. "If you'll just step outside a moment, the two of you, while the Missus and I do our business back here"—she pulls a curtain from the wall into a crescent around the bed—"you'll be surprised at what you see. Satisfaction guaranteed, right, Missus?"

My father and I step outside the curtain. From behind the white linen come the sounds of rubbing, pins being dropped, and the sleek whistle of a comb through wet hair. Mrs. Hull begins humming the tune I recognize from the day before. After a moment, my mother joins in, frail, tentative above the younger woman's voice. "That's right," Mrs. Hull says. "That's very pretty." They continue, Mrs. Hull a full, rich contralto, my mother a thin soprano, but stronger, more confident now. As they repeat the tune a few times through, she attempts a shy harmony, lapsing in and out of unison, perfecting her melody line. Beside me, without looking up, I sense my father shift his weight, transfer his coat from one arm to the other. We stand facing the curtain, not moving, and listen to the women sing.

NATALIE WOOD'S AMAZING EYES

I will not forget what Doug has given me. Not small things. When I clear out time to think about it, I know he has given me a lot.

Doug gave me the movies. I had always enjoyed them, but in a random, unspecific way. I would forget movies I had seen, and be just as willing to be terrified or sentimental the third time as the first. I didn't know names. It was the blonde with the hair over her face, or the one who looked like Spencer Tracy, but not exactly. Doug had books. He knew behind-the-screen stories. One of the first things Doug showed me was a picture of himself at a table with Martin Scorsese. It is quite a big table and Scorsese is all the way on the other side.

Doug has given me this house to live in. It is a ridiculous house; Doug's boss, Ernie Fike, built it for his bride, Mona. The automatic garage door plays "Amazing Grace" when it opens. There are mirrors over the bed and a ditch in the backyard where Fike was digging a pool. Fike's napkins say things like "To our wives and sweethearts. May they never meet." He has glasses decorated with women whose clothes disappear when you tilt them. In the bathroom, upstairs, the light switch is a woman's breast. You have to press the nipple to turn on the light. When I told Doug I didn't think I could touch it, he put a Band-Aid over the top.

Fike and Mona lived here six months before she ran off to Las Vegas. Fike told us to move in because the memories were too painful for him, but I'm sure it was the pictures. They still come, every week or so, each showing Mona with a different man. Sometimes they're having drinks on a veranda or toweling off after a dip in the pool. Most of the time, they're in bed. The men look like young doctors in the soaps, and Mona's eyes are closed and her head back, in every shot. Fike moved after Mona had some of the photos made into postcards. She wrote, "Thinking of you," and signed them, "Mrs. Ernie Fike." Fike swears he heard the postman giggle and two tellers talking about him at the bank. Since he doesn't want them, I keep the pictures, now. I look at Mona's clothes and try to see what she and her friends are drinking. I wonder if they're at The Sands or Caesar's Palace. I'm happy for Mona and would miss it if she stopped writing.

Fike says we can stay as long as we like it here. There is talk of a big promotion for Doug in the works and if things keep going well, Fike says, we'll be able to buy this house outright in no time at all.

We love them all, not just the famous or critically acclaimed. We've seen *Stella Dallas* six times, *Laura*, four. We laughed so hard at *The Palm Beach Story*, we made ourselves sick and had to leave. We know whole sections of *The Thin Man* by heart, though none of our friends are interested any longer, and certainly none are willing to come with us into Manhattan for the Nelson Eddy-Jeanette MacDonald operettas the Thalia puts on every summer. We've lost friends who've tired of our Spring Byington or Edward Arnold birthday parties, and I've been told point-blank that something must be wrong with anyone who gets so much from the movies, unreal and in the dark as they are.

Doug showed me where to look. In the beginning, he was patient, and there was all the time in the world. He loved it, that I'd go back with him a second or third time to the same movie, and when he told me things, I remembered. I remembered Bruce Dern's first appearance, *Wild River*, and Dustin Hoffman's, *The Tiger Makes Out*. We could cry, if we wanted, and afterwards we could talk or just be together, quietly. We were in the old place then, on the West Side. We walked for hours and hardly said a word, and the whole city was like a movie.

Doug's job is the break we needed. When I met him, he was carrying a case full of screenplays and talking of impossible things. Now, Fike treats him like a son and tells him there is always room at the top, for those who know how to climb.

When Doug was mentioned for a promotion, he began working nights. We talked it over, and I brought up our movies. Of course, I would never stand in Doug's way. Still, I was hurt when Doug didn't seem to realize what this would mean. I'm not sure what I would have said if he told me, "No, Caroline, I turned them down. The evenings are ours," but as we picked our way silently through our Salad Niçoise, I heard him say something like that over and over in my head.

Doug encourages me to go to movies alone. He still hangs the schedules over the breakfast table and puts arrows near the ones that shouldn't be missed. At night, if he's not too tired, we talk about the movies I've been to. When I told him I noticed an aborigine wearing Adidas in *Apocalypse Now*, he seemed pleased, so I've been telling him other things, some of them not true. I can't know how he misses the movies, Doug says. He likes to think about me there, and to know I'm happy.

We talk a lot, Doug and I, sometimes over the phone during the day. I tell him about my life. I tell him if we're going to stay in this house, certain changes must be made. I tell him the living room is all wrong, the kitchen too cluttered, not at all right for people of our sort. We talk about things to do in the city, things to draw me out of the house, my options. There's school, I could always finish school, and there's my old job at the clinic; there are any number of things I could do, Doug says. If I get serious, he wants to know. Just tell him and he'll make the time to discuss it.

I haven't told him this.

I've been going to Times Square, to the houses where they show movies all day. Some of these movies are decent, but most are kung fu or sex. I'm not going to say I go only to the worthwhile ones, either.

The theaters are wonderful. Huge caverns with balconies and footlights, felt seats, and massive curtains folded like sculpture to the sides of the screen. Many were built for vaudeville, and entering them you feel as if those days were preserved somehow, like when you turn on an old radio and expect to hear Harry James. It never wears off, the shock of coming in from the noise and the glare, the heat, to a cool dark chamber, hundreds of seats, shadows, eyes, cigarette ends. It's a separate world. The air is full of possibilities.

I sit there and watch the movies. Sometimes, they are

entertaining, spy movies with Charles Bronson or Clint Eastwood as a lean killer. Other times, I don't pay attention. From the dark around me come noises. There is snoring and whispering and from far off in the balcony, quiet sounds like crying. There are moans and the sound of lips on skin and sometimes, the frank spill of water on the floor. The air carries many smells, and though I stay for hours, I cannot grow accustomed to it. If I look around, there is movement by the walls, figures pass through the exit light's dull red.

I have had encounters in these theaters.

Once a man sat behind me and talked to me for a long while. I looked ahead but I was not watching the movie. When I didn't answer, he undid his pants and then I heard his breathing change. When he got up to leave, he pushed his hand through my hair and said, "Bitch."

Another time, I heard sirens and voices from the foyer. People dragged themselves to look. On the screen, a naked woman lay on the bed as two young men approached. When the noises grew louder, I went out, too. A man was sitting by the wall, under the movie posters with their frames of flashing lights, and where the top of his head should have been were only blood and white bits of bone. I could not take my eyes off him until a cop began to move us away. When he put a hand on my arm, I started to run. It was Columbus Circle before I could make myself stop.

Maybe I should have been talking to Doug. There are things it's his responsibility to know. I wanted to tell him about the man in pink, but I couldn't.

He was over six feet, dressed completely in pink, from boots to suit to wide-brimmed hat. He stood under the exit sign, black skin luminous, as if it were taking light out of the air. When he sat in the section next to mine, several rows ahead, the screen grew brighter for a moment, and I could see he was looking at me.

He moved into my section, a few rows in front. The climactic fight scene was beginning; bodies careened through the air and a samurai in a white robe watched from a hillside. The audience started to cheer. He stared directly at me, back almost full to the screen, openly, calmly, and when the samurai sent a severed head flying, the audience screamed, and he moved into the seat next to mine.

He stared, as if I was across the theater, still. He had a trim mustache and very white eyes and when the reflected light changed, they were all I could see of his face. A scent came from him that I had never smelled before, and I found myself wondering what it could be, his fragrance, watching to see if he would smile.

I sat there until he put a hand out and lifted my skirt. He did not move then, did not come closer or reach farther with his hand. He held the hem of my skirt up as if he would bend toward me, but he didn't. I felt the theater air wind up my thighs and I watched his face in the dark.

Afterwards, I stood on the street outside Doug's building. Many windows were blank, but on the fourth floor, I could see the lights in Doug's office. I stood on the street for several minutes debating whether to go up, and then for several more, willing Doug to the window. I left then, went home and to bed. When Doug returned later, I pretended I was asleep.

From now on, this is all I will remember:

In *The Searchers*, Natalie Wood has been made impure by living with the Indians. John Wayne traces her down to kill her but just at the end, something, maybe something in her amazing eyes, changes him. He takes her in his arms and says, "Let's go home, Debby."

In *Only Angels Have Wings*, Cary Grant is in love with Thomas Mitchell, but there's nothing he can do about it. When Mitchell is dying, Cary Grant lights a cigarette and puts it between Mitchell's lips, a parting kiss.

In *The Big Heat*, all the women are eliminated. Glenn Ford's wife is blown up and his daughter taken away. Gloria Grahame, in atonement, has her lovely face splashed with boiling coffee. She dies. When Ford returns to the squad room, not a woman left in his world, he says, "Keep that coffee hot, Hugo."

When Doug invites Fike and one of his girls for dinner, I serve heart. The cookbook describes it as "a homey treat." Slice the heart, across the grain, into quarter-inch pieces. Pour into ovenproof dish of boiling water. Add carrots, celery (with leaves), onion, salt (to taste), green peppers. Cook until tender, one and a half to two hours. Add, if you wish, lemon juice or dry wine. Goes well with rice or potato dumplings.

Doug, Fike, and Rhonda have drinks while I finish cooking. Doug told Fike to bring whatever he liked. He brought a bottle of scotch and a bottle of gin, two kinds of bourbon, light and dark rum, and a melon liqueur that Rhonda says is dreamy over ice cream. All the bottles have been opened, and Fike is showing Doug how to use the ice machine that freezes little plastic nudes into the cubes.

After I serve the food, Rhonda takes a bite and asks what it is. I tell her and she runs from the table. Doug looks down at his plate. I can see his face changing. Fike continues eating and says he knew right away. I go after Rhonda and Doug grabs my arm in the kitchen.

"What are you trying to do?" he says.

"I'm sorry," I say. "Wasn't it good?"

He is looking back at the table, where Fike has helped himself to more. "Ruin your own life, Caroline," my husband says. "Don't try to ruin mine."

Rhonda is all right after she washes her face a few times. Doug has cleared the table and Fike is freshening the drinks. He comes into the kitchen while I make the dessert.

"That wasn't a very nice thing to do to Rhonda," Fike says. "She's sensitive. She cries when dogs get killed on TV."

I add caramel to the sauce. This is the hard part, the cookbook says. It should simmer but must not boil. I bring the wooden spoon around slowly and watch the sauce for signs of trouble. Fike lifts his glass and makes breathing sounds as he drinks.

"I liked it, though," he tells me. "I like all the organs."

The sauce has started to thicken. I reduce the flame and bring the spoon around faster.

"That looks good, too," Fike says. "Let me help you."

Doug comes into the kitchen just as Fike puts a hand on my breast. I see Doug stop for a second, then take a carton of ice cream from the freezer. He returns to the living room, where Rhonda has started to sing. Fike pushes my breast in small circular motions.

"Is this helping, Caroline?"

The man in the ticket booth knows me, or says he does when I ask. He tells me the theater is closed for cleaning. They close every morning, for two hours, for cleaning. I tell him I just want to wait inside. He looks at the money I've put down and then at my clothes and hair. Harmless, he decides, and gets up to open the door.

The foyer is cool and I walk past the darkened movie posters into the theater. Dim lights shine from the front of the auditorium, and I can see that the carpeting and seats are green. The high walls are covered with gods and goddesses, Egyptian, by the look of them, that I have never been able to see until now. They carry fruit, animals, and dishes filled with fire toward the stage. Over the stage are a long boat, and the sun, and two elegant dogs crouching. It is all very well done, beautiful, I think, gilded except where the plaster walls have erupted in long ugly patches. The curtains are still drawn, and in the light I can see the screen is torn and stained, but in the dark I know it will be mended.

I find a spot in the first balcony, arrange my coat, and sit. A man is sweeping, but he soon finishes and I am left alone in the theater. Delicate sounds carry to me, soft rumbling and a fine hiss like a soothing voice whispering. The air is still in this massive room, but it can seem to be moving. It is easy to imagine in here. I scan the empty seats, row after row ready for the show to begin. The lights grow dim. They will be gathering now, waiting to get in, the men with the weak smiles and stunned eyes, lining up for the dark. I can see them in their coats, their wide-brimmed hats, walking up the carpeted hallway past the movie posters, now dazzling, toward the steel doors with the gold handles, toward the quiet and dark. I see them in flanks, in long shambling columns, coming to where I wait. Let them come to me.

THE ONLY THING YOU'VE GOT

There was a guy on the television one time, he'd written a book and had gotten used to seeing his picture in the papers. Donna and I had the color set in the bedroom then, and this guy had on a suit that looked borrowed. He held a pipe in his hand and pressed into the bowl with his thumb. He didn't smoke, which was probably not allowed on the set, but he looked like he wanted to. He would be all right, I suppose, if you met him on the street, but fame and glory had gone to his head, and you could tell he thought he had something to tell you about the way you were living your life. His book was about six generations in a New Orleans family, and the host asked him how he came up with that particular idea. The author sucked on the pipe once or twice, and looked into the camera. "It's a funny thing about family," the author said. "You spend your whole life wishing you didn't have any. Then there comes a time when you look around and realize it's the only thing you've got."

I was out of bed before he finished, and had punched the off button on the set. Donna was reading a magazine and waiting the eight minutes until she could take the ointment off her face. She looked up.

"What's that guy know about it," I said, pointing at the emptying picture tube. "What's he got to say to me?" I said, and went out the door to get a drink of water.

All this started with a phone call from my Uncle Phil earlier that night. I asked him about Toledo, and he asked me about my work, the weather. After the preliminaries, he said, "Joe. This thing I'm calling about is a favor. I've got a favor to ask you, Joey."

"That's okay, Phil," I said. "You can ask."

"It's your cousin. Margaret. You remember Margaret from the old days."

I told him I remembered.

"Well. She's married now, a fellow she met over at the college. They've got a kid, and the husband, his name is Howard, Joey, Howard has a good job lined up in Massachusetts. Deerfield, Massachusetts."

"What's Howard do, Phil?" I asked, so I could have something to say.

"Office machines. Office supplies. He's doing pretty good, Joe. I think he's in the office supplies line."

My Uncle Phil paused, and I could hear him sucking hard on a cigarette. I remember his face, and it was never without a cigarette stuck in it, like the cigarette was as much him as his nose was. My family told Phil every chance they got that cigarettes would be the death of him. When they finally were, two years after this conversation, I thought of calling various people in my family and asking them if they felt good, now that the tally was in. I thought about calling, but I never did.

Back on that night, anyway, I listened to Phil draw the smoke deep into his chest and I could almost see the look on him as the nicotine kicked into his blood. I thought of lighting one up myself, and right then I decided I'd do the favor for Uncle Phil's daughter, though I saw it all coming as clear as I ever saw anything in my life.

I remembered Margaret and her mother as hard, silly women who understood nothing about life except what they could get out of it. Phil's wife, Joline, came from a farming town in Indiana, where her father didn't own a farm, or much else, from what we heard. But to listen to her talk, you'd think he was governor of the state. Joline was a great one for advancement. She was always reading in the papers about somebody she used to know intimately who was now manager of a bank in Chicago or moving to the Coast to sell condominiums to movie stars. Every word out of her mouth somehow let you know Uncle Phil was not in the league of these acquaintances of hers. And when she talked, Phil got this look on his face like a man who's learned there's no arguing with the breaks.

My mother and Phil had been close their whole lives, and I never understood how Joline managed to come between them. When my mother died, Uncle Phil told me that for years, once or twice a month, they'd meet for lunch at a restaurant by the Michigan line and talk over old times. Nobody ever knew, Phil said, least of all Joline. But it was something he had with his sister, Phil said, something he still had, even with her gone.

The day we buried my mother was hot, in the nineties, and the weather sat on us all like a weight, making it an effort just to move. I hadn't had a clear thought in the two days since she'd died, except that I was out at the Road House with my buddies when it happened—I was twenty-two, and likely to be there as anyplace, I suppose—and I allowed myself to be led around by people, the reverend and his wife, the neighbors, from place to place, until they told me what to do next. I was in the living room while they brought the car around, and I heard Joline talking to her sister, who'd come in from St. Louis. I heard Joline tell her sister she could finally have that dining-room set, now Joline would be getting my mom's. I heard them discuss the end tables in the living room, and the portrait of my grandfather done by the Mason City Lions. When sister had to get up and go to the can, Joline followed. They were right in front of me and Joline said, "You still don't have a TV for the downstairs, do you?"

At the cemetery, heat vapors were lifting off the asphalt and the hoods of cars in the parking lot, steaming off the grass and changing the light between the trees. Mrs. Townsend, from the laundry, fainted, and had to be carried into the office. When the prayers were said and the body was in the ground, I stood by as people filed out. Most said something to me, some touched me on the shoulder. I stood there, not thinking a thought, just waiting, until I turned and walked fast out to the cars.

I found Joline supervising the loading of the flowers into her station wagon. I walked up quick, I was almost running, and she'd even turned to me with her mouth open when Phil grabbed me by the arm. He put himself between me and Joline and didn't let go. "I know what's in your head," he told me. "It ain't worth it." He held on to me until I shrugged him off and walked to my car. My insides were turning just like I'd been punched in the gut. I drove straight home, and was on an eastbound bus the next morning.

I remembered Margaret too, her mother's soul mate, and I'd moved 1,400 miles to get out of their line of fire. That's the way I thought about it when I told Donna this cousin of mine and her kid and husband would be staying with us for a day or two. I looked around the room, straightened a picture that had gone crooked, and I thought, you're okay. You've done pretty well so far.

I told Donna mostly about Phil, not about Margaret. I told her he was the one who showed me to keep two fingers out of a baseball glove to take off some of the impact, how to downshift instead of wearing out the brakes. I told her things like that. She smiled and said it would be nice, finally, to meet some of my family.

When we finished up that night I didn't move off her right away. I stayed there and held her. We didn't talk. Later, I thought I heard something and woke up. I didn't hear it again. I edged over as softly as I could and listened to my wife breathing, like at any second, she might stop for good.

They pulled up in a new Toyota wagon with a boxed bicycle on top. Margaret got out of the car holding this boy, about eight or nine, by the hand. Howard stayed behind the wheel for some reason, looking at the dash, and I wondered if they were having an argument.

Margaret came up the walk and I went to meet her halfway. I was getting set to put my arms around her shoulders or lean across to kiss her when she stopped and pushed the boy out in front of her.

"Andrew," she said. "This is Uncle Joe. This is Mama's cousin from when she was a little girl."

Andrew stood on the walk and I started out to shake his hand, but for some reason, I froze. I felt the back of my neck, like all of a sudden I knew someone was watching me from behind. He was a skinny boy with a bowl-shaped haircut, a white shirt smudged with dirt, and this bow tie that looked soaked in pickle brine. He was a bratty-looking unattractive kid, that's the truth, but that's not what got me. What got me was he looked at me without a hint of a smile, not the least bit of politeness in his face as we stood there in front of my home. He looked at me like he'd been told horror stories about me for his whole life and now he'd found out they were all true. In a man, I would have done something to a look like that, but coming from this little kid, I felt afraid. It passed, but for a minute, that's the way I felt.

Howard, at the car, was struggling to get the bicycle off the luggage rack. "Let me give you a hand with that," I called out, and I left the kid and his mother to find their own way inside.

Howard and I stored the new bicycle in the garage and carried the luggage indoors. Donna was showing Margaret the collection of snapshots we have over the fireplace, shots of me and Donna as kids next to pictures of our kid, Jennifer, in the same getup and poses. We've got me holding a bat over my left shoulder and Jenny holding one over her right, the two facing each other so they look like the same shot, except reversed. We've got the same deal with pictures of Donna and Jenny sitting at a table with a bunch of flowers. I spent some time getting the flowers to look the way they did in the old shot, and we even went out and bought Jenny a dress like the one Donna had, though if you look closely you can tell the colors aren't exactly right. It's not a big deal, really, just something we enjoyed among ourselves.

Donna had Margaret over by the pictures and I noticed, gratefully, that she had slipped upstairs and tied her hair in that way I like, looped over itself in a loose knot like you might do with a clip, but without one. I always loved it when she wore it that way and I looked at her with the long blond hair down her back and the curves to her waist and legs, and then I noticed she had put out coasters and a tray of crackers and cheese. I thought I should try to remember the feeling I was having just then.

Margaret, with her hands behind her back, moved from picture to picture like someone in a museum. The kid, Andrew, stood by this table we have with knickknacks on it, and kicked at the leg with his shoe. What kind of kid walks into a stranger's house and starts beating on the furniture, I said to myself. Then Howard, without a word, goes over and grabs the kid, hard, by the arm. He shakes him, then he lets him go. The kid moves a foot or so away and stops, not a sound out of him. Margaret doesn't even turn around.

"Let me get all of us a drink," I said, after Howard had joined his wife. I half expected Donna to give me a look, since it wasn't even two in the afternoon, but she was staring at the boy, Andrew, who stood in the middle of the room with his cheeks going bright red. "How about a drink?" I said again. "Howard, how's a beer sound? I've got Heineken and I've got light beer for the ladies."

Howard said a beer would be fine and went over to the sofa by the cheese tray.

"Margaret?" I said. "How about you?"

She put down a picture, out of order, and went to sit by her husband. "I wouldn't say no to a scotch," she said.

The boy came away from the knickknack table and sat by his mother. She piled some cheese on a cracker and handed it to him. He sat there, looking at it.

"How about you, Andrew?" I said. "Coke? Mountain Dew?"

165

"He likes that, don't you, Andrew?" Margaret said. "He's always asking for Mountain Dew."

"We don't keep any pop in the house," Howard told Donna. "We don't believe in it."

Donna looked at the boy. He glanced at her and then put his untouched cheese and cracker back on the coffee table. I noticed he dragged his hand along the slipcover when he'd put the food down.

"Andrew," Donna said, leaning toward him. "Pretty soon your cousin Jenny will be home and the two of you can play. Would you like that?"

In the kitchen, I arranged napkins on a tray, and five tall glasses. I got the can of Mountain Dew, one light beer, and two Heinekens from the refrigerator, and I put these on the tray next to the napkins. I put swizzle sticks on the tray, one for Margaret and one for the boy. I got the bottle of scotch from over the sink and poured a couple of fingers into Margaret's glass, and then I opened the freezer to get ice.

I stopped with my hand in the ice tray, cubes in my palm and around my fingers, the cold holding me there. I stood there, and in my head, I closed the freezer door and walked into the living room. I picked Howard up by the back of his collar and pushed him at the door. I screamed at Margaret to get out, all of them to get out of my house. This is my house, I screamed. I live here now. With my hand in the ice beginning to throb, I watched myself go up to Andrew and bury my fist in his boy-round face.

I was shaking a little when I closed my hand around a few cubes and shut the freezer door. I'd been holding these cubes in my hand, so I ran water over them before I put them in Margaret's glass. Then I filled another glass with water so

Margaret could suit her own taste. I wondered if I'd been in the kitchen too long and I tried to prepare a joke about it just in case. When I came into the living room, they were talking, Donna and Howard were talking and Margaret was listening to what they said. But the kid, Andrew, over by his mom with a new piece of cheese in his hands, he stared out from the rest of them directly at me, like he had been reading my mind all the time I was away.

Jenny came home from baseball practice and stood in the doorway all smudged and dusty and beautiful to look at while introductions were made. I'd had a beer or two by then, we'd all had a beer or two, and the first thing I felt like doing was going up to her, taking her out of the room and telling her the situation, saying there might be some trouble here and I hated putting any pressure on her, but I loved her, and we were in this together, weren't we, so what are you going to do? Donna guided Jenny to the boy. The two of them stood there and then Jenny reached out a hand and smiled, and I felt this warmness behind my eyes and I had to look away.

"Pleased to meet you," I heard her say.

"Isn't she something?" Margaret said. "Howard, look at these clothes. Dressed up just like a little boy."

Howard said, "Home from the ballpark?"

"We played Lincoln today."

"You hit any home runs?" Howard poured Heineken into his glass.

"Nope. Struck out twice and hit into a double play."

Howard sat back, satisfied, it seemed to me, and Jenny gave me a look. Forget it, I wanted to tell her. Go have dinner at Emily's. Daddy and Mommy will take care of this. She turned to Andrew, who was staring at her with the same look he'd used on me out on the front walk.

"You like horses?" she said to him.

"Of course I like horses." These were the first words we'd heard him say. "Who doesn't like horses?"

"I've got a collection."

"Where?"

"In my room. Upstairs, in my room."

"Could I look at them?"

"You can come up. We'll see about the horses later."

At the stairs, Jenny tossed her glove at Andrew, who put it on and began pounding his fist into it. We heard him say, "You play a position?"

"Catcher."

"Well, this isn't no catcher's mitt."

When they had gone, Margaret said, "Well. That is a striking little girl. You realize of course, Joe, who she's the very image of?"

"Who?" I said.

"Why, your grandmother. Our grandmother, I should say. She looks just like Grandmother in the old pictures."

"She looks a lot like Donna's mom," I said. "You wouldn't believe it if you saw them together. Everybody comments on it."

Margaret stirred her drink with a finger. Three swizzle sticks lay in a small puddle on the table.

"Well, she's got the good bones," she said. "That's a strong quality in our blood. Doesn't she have that quality, Howard?"

"I don't know," Howard said. "I'm not a big one on bones. What grade is she at school?" he asked Donna.

"She's in the fourth grade," I said. "She goes to the

Roosevelt School just two blocks away. It's a well-known school around here."

Howard turned to me. He was a little guy and nervous. By the way his skin was tight on his face, you could tell that he pulled at it with his jaw muscles. He had a way of staring you right in the eye that said, "You think I'll back down on this one, but you've got a surprise coming." He looked at me that way.

"Andrew's in the sixth grade," he said. "They pushed him a grade ahead. His principal said he has a remarkable mind and a special aptitude for abstract conceptualization."

Over on the other side of the room, Donna let out a laugh. Both Howard and Margaret turned to her.

"That's not my thinking," Howard said. "Those were the principal's exact words."

Donna took a sip of beer and brought a hand to her cheek, lovely now with a high color in her face.

"I'm sorry," she said. "I'm sure that's very nice."

Howard sat straighter on the sofa and didn't say anything. Donna glanced at me. She said, "Well, you could tell the moment you look at him that he's an intelligent child. I could see that almost immediately."

Margaret said, "He's never got less than a ninety-six on any arithmetic test," and then she smiled and held out her empty glass.

"Oh, here," Donna said. "Let me get that, Margaret. I'm in need of a fresh one myself."

When Donna had gone into the kitchen, I said, "Folks, I was thinking of grilling up some steaks this evening, seeing as how this is a family get-together. Why don't you go upstairs when you're ready? I'll show you the room and the bathroom, if you like. There's plenty of hot water if you don't

169

take too many showers in a row, but me and Donna are all set in that department."

They got their drinks and I led them upstairs. In their room, Donna had laid out towels, two neat stacks by the foot of the bed. She had put water glasses on the dresser and opened the windows, and the breeze blew the curtains into the room and the whole place was clean and neat and filled with light.

"Here you go," I said. "Now, take your time. Whenever you're ready, we'll see about those steaks."

On the way downstairs, I stuck my head in Jennifer's room. The two kids were on the rug and Jenny's famous collection of plastic horses was spread out all over. Andrew had a horse in his hand and was making it rear up on its hind legs and whinny. Jenny laughed at this and then she saw me. The look she gave me was so easy and free of concern that I went downstairs shaking my head, wondering what my problem was.

I fired up the grill slowly, and looked around. It was a fine summer evening and there was this calm in the air and in the light over the houses. Someone had already barbecued down the street, and the smell hit me, like the daylight and the leaves turning in the wind. It was a day to make you stop and take notice.

I'd driven to the supermarket and spoken to the butcher personally about the steaks. He was a heavyset man about my age, with his hair neatly parted under his white hat. We talked for a few minutes about the price of meat and the best cuts and this marinade he knew about. He was a friendly guy who seemed happy in his work, and after we talked, I carried the meat in the orange paper, and the packages felt good in my hand. Just seeing them on the seat next to me on the drive home made me feel better, too.

Howard came out and started cutting up potatoes for fries. Then Donna and Margaret brought the tray with more drinks, and we set up chairs on the lawn and sat around talking. From the upstairs window, you could hear the kids laughing, and the steaks lay soaking in the butcher's marinade, and it seemed everything might turn out all right in the end.

"Hope nobody's dying out here," I said. "The coals are almost ready."

"Maybe I'll put Andrew's new bicycle together, then," Howard said. "If there's enough time before dinner."

"Should be," I said. "I'll give you a hand."

When I came out of the garage with my tool kit, Howard was staring at the bicycle spread out on the ground.

"I didn't think it would have so many parts," he said. "There aren't any instructions."

We started going at it piece by piece, the two of us, but when Howard saw I had the exact tool for ratcheting the handlebars into place and that I knew to adjust the individual spokes to true the wheel rotation, he backed off and watched me work. I wouldn't have minded help from Howard, but I knew I'd do it better and faster if I were left to it myself.

After I aligned the wheels, I poked around in the gear box for a while. I lubricated the chain and the brake lines, and I thought of opening the bracket and headset to get a look at the ball bearings, but decided that would be going too far. I coiled tape carefully along the handlebars, and I told Howard to get new brake shoes, racing-type, first chance he got. I adjusted the seat, and to finish it off, went over the frame with some auto paste wax to protect the paint job. It wasn't for the kid. I just liked to do things right back then.

By the time I was finished, Donna had laid out the plates and the food, and she warned me it was all getting cold. I

171

told them to start, and Howard and I went into the house to wash up.

"We'll let Andrew take her for a spin after we eat," I said.

Howard said, "How come I don't see any bikes around here?"

"I don't know," I said. "Guess I just lost interest. I don't even think Jenny's ever been on one."

I backed away from the sink to let Howard in, and wiped my hands with the towel on the door. He washed his hands with a lot of energy, as if there was something on them to wash off. Over his shoulder, he told me, "Andrew is a very advanced rider. He's been riding two-wheelers since he was five years old."

The steaks were fine quality, and if they'd been left to cool too long, no one seemed to mind. The light was still high over the houses, even after the sun went down through the trees, and someone said sometime this week was the longest day of the year. We ate the steaks and a salad and Howard's fries, and we all had another drink. The bike, shiny-new, red paint and chrome and black tape, lay handsomely on the lawn, and it gave me a good feeling just to look at it.

The conversation went this way and that, and I tried not to pay attention as much as I could. Then Howard and Margaret got back on Andrew, their favorite topic, and I came around. I wasn't used to people talking about their kids with the kids sitting right in front of them.

"Many of Andrew's teachers advise us to look into a special school for him. They say a career in public service or in the advanced sciences is probably what he's destined for." This was Margaret talking, waving her glass in the air. "Mrs. Thatcher, in the fourth grade, said Andrew was the most remarkable student she'd had in seventeen years' teaching."

Howard said, "He reads everything, even high school text-books. Last year, he read *Catch-22*, didn't you, son?"

The kids were sitting on the grass, and Donna had laid out a plastic tablecloth for them. Andrew was still in the same grimy getup he'd walked in wearing, though there'd been plenty of time to change. He looked at his father and said, "Yes. It was an interesting book."

"Did you like it?" Donna said. "I read that book. What did you like about it, Andrew?"

The kid put down his fork and looked at my wife as if a pretty patient woman trying to make simple conversation was just about more than he could take.

"The irony," he said. "I enjoyed the irony."

The irony. I was all set to ask the kid just what in the hell that was supposed to mean, but Margaret cut me off.

"He's always using those words, isn't it a kick in the pants? One time, I did something, I don't know what, something Andrew didn't like. So what did he say? He said I was exasper-ating him. Exasperating, could you believe it?"

I went over to the ice chest and pulled out a beer for myself. I didn't ask if anybody else needed one.

"Jennifer's got a lead in the spring play." I heard it and couldn't believe it was my voice. "They chose her because she can sing rings around any kid in that school."

Howard nodded, and I could feel Donna looking at me from the side, but I went on. "The drama coach said there were over three hundred lines in the part, and she's only got two weeks to learn all of them."

Margaret smiled. "Andrew would love to be in a school play, I'm sure. He's just got so little time with his studying and his outside reading and Debating Club."

"Jenny was on the Debating Club," I said. "Last year. And

173

the Computer Club and the Young Students for Civic Health Club, or something like that. Weren't you, doll? Tell these people if I'm talking through my hat."

I had walked over to my chair on the lawn, but I didn't sit. I looked at Jenny but she had her face turned away. All I could see was the striped back of her halter top, and the blond hair, straight, like her mom's, parting around a freckled shoulder. I couldn't see the freckles from where I was, but I knew they were there, and it was just like seeing them. Then I looked over at the kid, Andrew, and he was staring up at me like I'd just been announced as the greatest fool in America.

"Hey, Andrew," I said. "You're done with dinner. Why don't you ask your folks if you can try out that new bike?"

"Yes," Margaret piped up. "Of course you can. Why don't you take it for a test drive? And then ask your cousin Jennifer if she'd like to try."

"She can't ride," Howard said.

The kids got the bike and Andrew led it to the low wall framing the neighbor's garden. He stood on the wall and lifted his leg, and then he was over the seat and on his way. I glanced at Donna for one second and she was watching me. There was a lot in that stare, I know now, and I knew it then, but all I could see at that moment was the set of her jaw, and her eyes, staring at me just like the kid had done. I didn't look at her again.

The bike worked fine. Andrew rode it to the end of the block and back, waving at us as he went by. He came back in the other direction, riding in the street now, and he lifted his hands off the bar. Margaret waved. When he came by a third time, I was there in the street to meet him. He stopped the bike just in front of me.

"Why don't you give your cousin a chance?" I said.

"She can't ride."

"She can ride," I said. "Just get off before I knock you off."

He gave me the bike, biting both lips between his teeth. I held the handlebar stem in my fist and wheeled the bike to where they were all sitting.

"C'mon, baby," I said to Jenny. "You wanna try?"

"Joe," Donna said.

"I'll hold you, doll. I'll hold you the whole way."

"Joe." Donna put a hand on my shirt. "She's never been on one before."

I spoke without looking at her. "You don't think she can do it?" I said. "You don't think she can ride a goddamned bicycle, for God's sake?"

Donna took her hand off and walked away. I knelt on the grass in front of Jennifer.

"Whad'ya say, gorgeous? You wanna go for a ride with your old man?"

I held the bicycle steady by the neighbor's wall as Jenny climbed onto the seat. She put a hand on my belt at first, but I had the handlebars in one hand and the back of her seat in the other, and as we moved out to the sidewalk, she let go of me.

I leaned into her and spoke. "We'll go as slow as you like, baby. Just as slow as you like. I'll be here the whole time."

The bike was too big for her, it was too big for both of the kids. But if she shifted her weight, she could reach the pedals, and after a couple of misses, we were moving right along the street. We picked up some speed, and the houses to either side, all familiar to me at a walk, seemed changed. I took my hand off the seat and put it on my daughter's shoulder. I could feel the sweat on her sunburned skin, and inside, I could feel the bones working. I let go.

175

She did fine for two houses, three. I thought she was going to make it but her front wheel turned all of a sudden and she was dumped off the bike, half on a neighbor's lawn, half on the sidewalk.

I could tell by the way she lay there that she was all right. I could tell from the way her legs bent at the knees and the way her arms were out at her side that she was just resting, just getting her wind. I knew she was okay, and I wanted to say that to Donna as she ran by me on the grass, but I didn't. When Donna picked her up and they came walking back to the house, I could see I'd been right, but I didn't say anything then, either. They just walked by me, Donna and Jennifer did, and they didn't stop. I went to the corner past the short skid mark where she'd had her fall. I reached the corner and kept going. I made a wide circle through the neighborhood, past the shops on the boulevard, the co-ops, the municipal playground. When I came back not too much later, the bike was out of sight and they'd cleaned up all the food and plates. All the doors were closed too, and the blinds, and I stood there in front of my house wondering what I would do next.

Understand this about Donna. She came into my life like one of the three wishes, like a winning lottery ticket, like a miracle I didn't even know I needed. And I never forgot that. Even now I haven't forgotten. She came in like a miracle to my life, and for a while between us, everything was possible.

I'm not simple enough to say that afternoon with my cousin Margaret and her weird kid was what did it to me and Donna. Or even to say it all started with that. I don't understand any more about it now than I did when it all came apart, of my own doing—I understand that much—or when all the turns I might have made to save myself were passed over, one by one by one.

In the meantime, my Uncle Phil kicked off, hacking and blowing smoke in their faces to the end. I got my inheritance in the mail—two Swiss-type pipes with little guys with beards on the bowls, and like the pictures I get sent of Jenny at the prom, Jenny at her driving lesson, Jenny on a diving board in Fort Lauderdale, I try not to look at them.

One thing stays with me though, and I've no accounting for it. There was a moment, just a couple of seconds, between when I let go of Jenny that day, and when she lay without moving on the grass. It was like this. I had her in my hands. I had both hands on her small shoulders and I could feel their strength. Her hair was coming up slowly behind her, catching the wind, and I could hear the tires snaking on the sidewalk and the sound our breathing made. I could see everything, the houses, the cars, the gardens with their flowers and rock beds, and when I let go of her, just for a moment, it was like she'd left the ground, like she'd taken off quietly into the trees. And on the entire planet, only I was there to see it.

About the Author

EHUD HAVAZELET was born in Israel and raised in New York City. He was educated at Columbia University, the University of Iowa Writers Workshop, and Stanford University, where he held a Wallace Stegner Fellowship. His stories have appeared in *The North American Review*, *The Missouri Review*, *The Ontario Review*, and *The Iowa Review*, and he has been anthologized in *20 Under 30*, published by Scribners, and *The New Generation*, published by Doubleday. He has recently been named a fellow at the Cité Internationale des Arts in Paris. Currently he is a Jones Lecturer at Stanford University and lives with his wife in Palo Alto, California.